"I sho

To his brightly, "You're right. Here I am being nosy, when you're just thinking about doing your job."

"No."

In the act of pushing back her chair, she went still. Her eyes searched his.

"You have to know—" Damn, his throat felt like it was full of gravel, and his voice sounded as if it was, too. Somehow he'd come to be standing.

"Know what?" she whispered, rising to her feet.

"You're more than a job." Oh, that was eloquent.

Eyes wide, she waited.

"I'd like to kiss you."

Her eyes dilated and she moistened her lips before she said, "I'd like that. Although..."

"Although?"

STORING SECRETS

JANICE KAY JOHNSON

Harlequin
INTRIGUE

Harlequin®
INTRIGUE™

ISBN-13: 978-1-335-69011-1

Storing Secrets

Copyright © 2025 by Janice Kay Johnson

Harlequin Enterprises ULC
22 Adelaide St. West, 41st Floor
Toronto, Ontario M5H 4E3, Canada
www.Harlequin.com

Printed in Lithuania

Recycling programs
for this product may
not exist in your area.

MIX
Paper | Supporting
responsible forestry
FSC® C021394

An author of more than ninety books for children and adults with more than seventy-five for Harlequin, **Janice Kay Johnson** writes about love and family and pens books of gripping romantic suspense. A *USA TODAY* bestselling author and an eight-time finalist for the Romance Writers of America RITA® Award, she won a RITA® Award in 2008. A former librarian, Janice raised two daughters in a small town north of Seattle, Washington.

Books by Janice Kay Johnson

Harlequin Intrigue

Visit the Author Profile page at Harlequin.com.

CAST OF CHARACTERS

Erin Reed—A young single mother who has made a living by buying secondhand goods from storage unit auctions and garage sales, Erin discovers something terrible in one of the tubs of goods.

Jeremy Conyers—Having recently inherited a storage facility, Jeremy discovers his uncle hadn't kept decent records in years. When a black-masked man batters him and sets a fire to kill him, Jeremy is saved by Erin Reed—but not until he's given the attacker her name, along with others.

Sam McKeige—A detective who has blocked out the tragic loss of his son, Sam discovers he'll do anything to protect Erin and her boy, Toby.

Toby Reed—A sunny-natured three-year-old boy who brings painful memories back to Detective McKeige but who also teaches him to love again. If only a killer didn't intend to use Toby to terrorize his mother.

Chapter One

The small cluster of people—four of them in addition to Erin Reed—stared into the packed ten-by-fifteen-foot storage unit. A few feet from Erin, her three-year-old son sat cross-legged on the asphalt, drawing a picture with colored chalk. For a child his age, he was exceptionally patient.

Erin didn't know how she'd have managed if Toby weren't so good at entertaining himself.

Thank goodness Jeremy Conyers, the new owner of this storage facility, didn't seem to mind the chalk. Of course, it would wash off with the next rain, never far away in western Washington. Right now, Jeremy just stood there waiting with his arms crossed. He'd probably conducted enough of these auctions to be able to guess what he'd make for the contents of the units. No doubt he was more excited that whoever won the auction would have to haul all the junk away, allowing him to rent the unit again.

Erin knew that all too often, people spent an awful lot of money to store battered furniture and boxes of used clothing and kitchenware in just decent enough shape to be donated to a thrift shop.

"Three hundred," one guy said without a lot of enthusiasm.

"Three fifty," someone else countered.

Having no intention of bidding this time, Erin pondered why people always deposited their unwanted washers and dryers at the front of a storage unit. Pile a few plastic tubs atop them, and the aging appliances did an excellent job of blocking any view of whatever was stored deeper inside a space that was usually longer than wide.

Erin's livelihood was based on her keen eye. She hit up every garage sale in surrounding towns and judged how high to bid on the contents of storage lockers that went up for auction after the owner quit paying the bills. Her judgment was good enough to support herself and her son without having to pursue Toby's dad through the courts. That might mean actually having to *see* him again.

She knew all of the other bidders here today casually, at least. Two of them sold solely on eBay. One claimed he did, but he usually shied away at the last minute and got outbid, so who knew? She was the only one of the small group who both sold online and had a good-sized booth in an antique mall here in town.

"Four hundred," offered Kevin Hargrave—no, Hargrove, Erin thought.

She kept her mouth shut, and after a few grimaces, so did everyone else. The auction ended there. Kevin and Jeremy huddled for a moment over a clipboard before Jeremy closed the unit door and handed the key to the padlock to Kevin.

As always, Erin crossed her fingers that she hadn't passed up a treasure trove. Her last glance at what she could see reassured her.

A lanky man in his early thirties who'd inherited this independently owned storage facility from an uncle who'd recently died, Jeremy led the group around the end of the cinder-block strip of units to a second one, the contents of which were also up for auction.

Having two in one day was unusual, and Erin hoped things moved briskly. Toby might have an extraordinary attention span for a boy his age, but it wasn't unlimited. When she smiled and held out her hand, he clutched his chalk and trotted along at her side.

"How come you didn't buy that one?" he asked.

"Just...didn't see anything exciting," she explained.

He nodded. Apparently, he hadn't, either. At least he'd learned that he wasn't allowed to sneak in while the adults were occupied.

Jeremy unlocked this padlock and rolled up the blue door. "Fifteen by twenty-five feet," he told them.

That was about as big as these units came. The contents of an entire *house* could fit into that space.

Erin's attention sharpened, and she wasn't even sure why. The requisite washer and dryer sat in front, although these were in good enough condition they actually might be salable. Nobody was allowed to step into a unit, so they all wandered side to side, craning their necks, even rising on tiptoe. The peculiar shapes under tarps, packing blankets and sheets suggested furniture, although she could see some piles of plastic tubs, too. The most expensive kind, she noted, the ones that wouldn't crumple even if you jumped up and down on them.

A few inches of wood peeked out here and there, and wasn't that the neck of a musical instrument case? A guitar? No, she thought; something larger.

A hum of energy in the air told her she wasn't alone in her interest, although she also wasn't alone in maintaining an expression of skepticism on her face. *Nothing interest-*

ing here, she tried to project. On the plus side, those who sold solely online were less inclined to be interested in furniture, especially large pieces that were hard to store, package and ship.

Bidding started at five hundred but climbed quickly. Erin prided herself on knowing when to stop, but even when they passed five thousand dollars, she kept going. At eighty-five hundred, her principal competitor, Walt—something ordinary, like Jones or Smith—shook his head and said, "It's all yours. But, damn, I'd like to see what's in there."

She grinned at him. "You and me both. You wouldn't begrudge me a victory dance, would you?"

He laughed. "For that price, you might find yourself weeping, you know."

Unfortunately, that was true.

She signed her name on Jeremy's paperwork and accepted the key, then smiled at Toby. "Let's go get our truck, and we can take some stuff home with us now."

"Yeah!"

The group all walked back to the entrance together. She took the time to write a check to Jeremy and usher Toby to the bathroom before they drove back to unit 417.

After raising the door, she heaved several heavy plastic tubs to the back of her pickup truck, then used her dolly to laboriously move the dryer onto the asphalt surface in front of the storage unit to clear the way. Wiping the sweat from her face with a rag, she grimaced.

Why were the unwanted washers and dryers always at the front? Dumb question. The damn things were heavy and awkward. Why move them an inch farther than you had to? And, hey, if some rainwater seeped under the rolling door, who cared if the dented and/or rusting appliances were further damaged?

Excitement bubbled even as she pressed her hand to her aching lower back and turned to see what treasures she might have acquired.

Toby grabbed a handful of his mother's sweatshirt and didn't move. "Mommy?" He was usually eager to rush in.

Please don't let there be taxidermy elk heads meant to hang on the wall or other horrors.

She looked down to see his attention riveted on the jam-packed interior of the large unit. Her gaze followed his.

The furniture was mostly covered and had more plastic tubs and cardboard boxes piled atop, but…

A sheet had slipped off to reveal the incredibly elaborate top of what had to be a chest of drawers. She'd never seen anything like it outside of a museum. Below a soaring clam-shell top were rows of drawers covered with painted—or was that japanning?—animals and even tiny scenes. The leopard seemed to be staring straight back at Toby.

"What is it?" the little boy whispered.

"It's, well, I think it's a chest of drawers, like you have. Except…" Not.

Feeling as if she were dreaming, she squeezed her way past a table that, when she uncovered it, appeared to be cherry or rosewood, every line elegantly curved, the feet perfectly defined claws gripping balls. The chair…yes, there was one…matched. The sage green upholstered seat was covered in plastic and seemed to be in pristine condition.

She banged her shin against a cast-iron stove decorated more elaborately than a wedding cake. More furniture: an astonishing bookcase, a grandfather clock, a china cabinet she thought was from the Eastlake period. At the back stood a wardrobe of dark wood inlaid with flowers.

Despite the packing blankets, sheets and tarps that had been used to protect the furniture, dust lay everywhere. She opened a cracked leather case to find a cello with a bow. Everywhere she turned were antiques, and not common ones, either.

I'm rich, she thought, dazed. Who on earth could have stored nineteenth- and even eighteenth-century pieces of furniture of this quality in an ordinary storage unit in a small town off the highway that led to a Cascade Mountain pass in Washington state? Not exactly the antique hub of the universe, although she did well at the antique mall thanks to the travelers, skiers and hikers who got off the highway for a meal and a search for what they assumed had to be good deals this far off the beaten track.

Blinking, she whirled to look for Toby. He was trustworthy, of course he was, at least for his age, but—

With his small hand, he was gently moving an astonishing painted rocking horse. Oh, heavens…he would want it, and lord only knew how much it was worth. Would there be other toys in here?

"That's pretty, isn't it?" she said.

"Uh-huh. Would it *break* if I got on?"

"I…don't know. Why don't we wait until we get it home?"

He bit his lips but nodded.

She smoothed back his fine, light brown hair that she'd let get too long. "You know what? Let's load up as much as we can get in the pickup truck. I can hardly wait to see what's in all those boxes."

"Can we take this?" He petted the neck of the rocking horse.

"You bet." She smiled down at him, then picked the thing up and carried it out. She spread a packing quilt from the pile she always carried and wrapped the child's horse carefully before positioning it to one side of the bed. Once it was surrounded by boxes, it wouldn't be able to slide around.

Resisting the temptation to peek into some of those boxes was hard, but the sky had taken on an ominous cast. She didn't have a canopy on her truck because she often used it to haul furniture, so she definitely wanted to get home and unload before the rain started.

Toby did do a little poking as she worked, excitedly coming up with some tin toys that looked to be in beautiful condition. Still, he didn't argue when she repacked them and put that box, too, in the bed of the pickup.

Seeing the wonder on his face, she cursed his father for the twenty or thirty thousandth time. How could he have ditched his son as well as her? Did he know what he was missing? Her only consolation was that Toby was a happy kid who didn't throw temper tantrums and enjoyed browsing garage sales with her and figuring out how best to display items in her booth at the antique mall.

After lowering the rolling door, she locked it with a new, sturdier padlock to replace the one that had been on it for years. She buckled Toby into his car seat, although he was almost too big for it, and drove to the storage facility exit, where she input the code Jeremy had given her. Toby chattered during the fifteen-minute trip home, but for once she let a lot of what he said go in one ear and out the other.

Exhilaration still bloomed in her chest, but anxiety coiled around it. The stuff in that unit was too valuable. Who had stored it in the first place? Had somebody died, and heirs didn't know what was in there or that they needed to keep paying the monthly fee for the unit? Legally, Erin thought she was in the clear to start selling its contents, but ethically…she was less certain.

She ought to be gloating.

She was.

It was just that an inconvenient conscience had kicked in.

Mostly, she was unnerved by today's discoveries. Some things were too good to be true. She'd probably find the furniture were all modern reproductions. Worth quite a bit, even so, but that would be disappointing. Still, she wasn't even sure she knew *how* to sell items as fine as those if they were genuine. Did she have room to store them at home? And…what if some of those boxes contained smaller items just as exceptional?

What was more, she had two other storage units to clear out this week, one at the same facility. She'd barely glanced inside it. She was on such a roll, it would be smart to skip other upcoming auctions she'd usually attend in the area.

Right. As if she could resist.

Maybe, though, she should call Jeremy to ask if he'd either try to contact the former owner of this stuff or give her the name so she could get in touch herself.

Yes, that would make her feel better.

TWO WEEKS LATER, Erin was beginning to think she'd gotten in over her head. No, she hadn't been able to resist attending those other auctions. Or winning yet another one that her gut told her would be worthwhile.

She'd had so many units to empty, she needed to hire two local guys to haul everything back to her house. The garage was bulging at the seams. Overflow had long since spilled into her little-used dining room, then the living room. Honestly, she could no longer remember what had come from which unit at what facility—except for the truly extraordinary pieces of furniture from Jeremy's place.

She'd gone so far as to list what she'd decided definitely was a japanned highboy on eBay. Bids had blown her away—until a curator at the J. Paul Getty Museum in southern California messaged her. Erin agreed to let the woman look at the piece. She flew up the next day and bought the dresser for an amount of money that would pay for at least the first year or two of Toby's college education. Erin probably could have gotten more for it from a private collector, the curator was honest enough to tell her, but Erin liked the idea of this handsome piece displayed for the public. In return, the woman offered advice on how to sell a couple of the other pieces. Erin took down the eBay listing and found herself hesitating about the rest of the furniture and the cello.

Her conscience was knocking again. It became especially insistent at bedtime, as did her other worries.

She had to get some—all right, *a lot*—of the stuff from other units sorted and out of the house before she or Toby were buried by a falling tower of boxes.

The trouble was, it took time to research every item, take adequate photographs and write appealing and accurate descriptions. She strove to be transparent as a seller, so that nobody could later complain they'd been misled. If an item had a scratch on it, she described it and showed it in a photo. If the expected maker's mark didn't look quite right, she said so. Either way, she displayed it in a clear photo.

An item as small as a ring or silk scarf took as long as a chest of drawers, which meant that she could spend a day on the contents of a single plastic tub. She wouldn't make a lot of progress at that speed.

She refused to shortchange Toby, either. When he needed her to stop what she was doing and kick a ball in the backyard or read to him, she did. The financial windfall let her send him for a few extra hours a week to daycare, but while he didn't argue when she dropped him off, he wasn't excited, either. Maybe she needed to consider the two larger daycares in town, one part of a chain, one operated by a church. Toby needed more time with kids his age.

After all Erin's brooding that night, she whimpered when her alarm went off the next morning. She had too much to do, but she'd start with going back to the storage facility to talk to Jeremy in person. She couldn't figure out why he was making excuses rather than tracking down whoever had paid rent on that unit for heaven knew how many years. God forbid he give her a name. Didn't he get that she was trying to do the right thing? Why was that a problem for *him*?

Breakfast consisted of frozen waffles, toasted and buttered with no syrup for Toby, butter *and* syrup for her. Super nutritious, but she was too tired to cook this morning, and the waffles were Toby's favorite. He chattered happily between bites.

After swallowing the last of her tea, she said, "I have to go talk to someone this morning. Then I'm taking some stuff to the antique store. Marsha called to say enough has sold to open some room. If you'd rather go play with friends at Mrs. Hall's—"

The three-year-old shook his head. "I don't like Julia. I don't want to play with her."

"But Austin will be there—"

"Uh-uh. *He* said he didn't have to go there anymore."

Austin, not quite a year older than Toby, had been the main draw. Erin hoped Austin hadn't been telling the truth. She'd call Mrs. Hall later to find out. For now...

"Coming with me might be boring," she warned.

"I like going with you best, Mommy," he assured her with his usual heartfelt sincerity.

She grinned at him. "Then let's do it."

Half an hour later, she was waiting while Jeremy Conyers rented a U-Haul truck to an older woman.

"You bought the contents," he growled the minute he stepped foot back inside the office. "What's your problem?"

"I told you! I just can't believe family would have let such beautiful pieces go if they'd known—"

"Uncle Charles sent repeated bills. I sent a final one. They had their chance."

"Will you please check with them? Surely you have a phone number or address?"

He groaned. "Only the mailing address. Uncle Charles's records are a mess. He was getting a little confused toward the end. You know that."

Erin did. "From the layers of dust, I think this stuff's been in the unit for years. Older records—"

The lanky, frustrating young man she was facing yanked at his hair. "I still don't get—"

A familiar tug on the hem of her sweatshirt drew her attention downward to Toby. "I gotta go," he told her.

She summoned a smile. "Okay." She glanced back at Jeremy. "We need to use the restroom."

"You know where it is," he said. It was clear she was beginning to annoy him.

She led Toby to the single bathroom behind the office.

Jeremy kept it cleaner than his uncle had. The building also had a garage for maintenance equipment and a golf cart Jeremy used to zip around the facility. Whether he'd wanted to inherit the business or intended to sell it, she had no idea. Whoever was on duty in the office could see people coming and going through the gate, as well as watch security monitors covering the rows of rental units. Out of the corner of her eye, she saw at least three people parked in front of units, either loading or unloading.

A small plastic stool in the bathroom allowed Toby to stand high enough to use the toilet without her lifting him. Once he finished and she let him flush, she moved the stool in front of the sink so he could wash his hands. At home, he handled all this himself, but she wasn't ready to send him off alone in public places. Besides, he would skip hand-washing when he could get away with it.

"If I play in my sandbox, I'll get dirty again," he told her as she dried his hands with a paper towel.

She rolled her eyes, opened her mouth...and went still. What was she hearing?

It was coming from the office, only a wall away. Raised voices, metallic slams that must be file cabinet drawers and then a big crash.

She turned off the water and made sure Toby was looking at her and paying attention. "Shush. Stay *right* here. Promise me?"

Looking scared, he nodded.

She felt scared, too, but cracked the bathroom door anyway.

"Where's my stuff?" a man's voice snarled. "Tell me."

Oh, dear God. A black-clad figure who had his back to her was kicking Jeremy, who huddled on the floor among sliding heaps of paperwork and folders. Now the intruder lifted a baseball bat and swung. The distinct *crack* she heard had to be the sound of bones breaking.

"Where? Who has it? You have to know!"

Crack.

Jeremy screamed, then started to babble names. Kevin Hargrove's jumped out at her. Why include him?

"Erin Reed!" Jeremy whimpered.

Erin covered a gasp with her hand. What if he said, *She's here right now. In the bathroom. If you want to ask her about anything.*

The man in black went back to ripping folders from the file cabinets and throwing them around the office, even on top of Jeremy who curled up with his arms protecting his head.

Erin shrank back but had to watch. After seeing what should have been the terrifying man's profile, she realized that he wore a ski mask.

"Mommy?"

She whirled and clapped her hand over his face. Toby's teeth chattered, and after he saw the fierce expression on her face, he started to cry. There was no way out of here except back through the office. If she or Toby caught the attention of this monster, she had a bad feeling they'd both die.

Jeremy wasn't moving anymore. For a moment, the man stood above him staring down. Then he took something from his pocket and flicked it with a finger.

Already terrified, she didn't see the first lick of flame until papers on the floor caught fire.

Chapter Two

When the black-clad man flung open the door and walked out, the rush of fresh air fed the fire, flames leaping higher.

Shaking all over, Erin made herself stay where she was. She could just see a slice of the parking lot in front of the office through the window. A dark SUV appeared, backing out, swinging in a circle and, an instant later, accelerating too fast onto the two-lane road in front of the storage facility.

She whirled, snatched up Toby and ran with him into the burning office. "Jeremy!"

He whimpered and tried to push himself to his hands and knees but slumped back to the floor. He had to feel the heat of the approaching flames.

"Oh God. Oh God." Erin didn't want to let go of her sobbing little boy, but she couldn't leave Jeremy to burn to death, either. She raced to the exterior door, planted Toby right in front of it, and dodged the fire racing back through the scattered papers to reach Jeremy.

Somehow, she'd never know how, she got her arms around him and began to drag him toward the door. He had to weigh significantly more than she did, but she kept him moving anyway. The heat singed her face and licked at his pants leg.

Toby was distraught, and she probably was, too, by the time she got the door open, pushed the little boy ahead of her, and nearly fell through with Jeremy. She paused to stomp out the fire smoldering on the leg of his chinos, then descended the concrete stairs with his feet bumping behind her.

"Mommy!" Toby whimpered. "Mommy!"

A few more feet. She had to make it a few more feet. The concrete building wouldn't burn, but the roof might.

Then she heard a shout. A car door slammed, and two men ran toward her. One lifted Jeremy and slung him over a shoulder, the other grabbed Toby and took Erin by the hand as they ran a safe distance away.

As Erin collapsed to her butt on the gritty asphalt, reaching for her son, one of her rescuers called 9-1-1.

By the time Sam McKeige arrived at the storage business on the outskirts of town, the fire was out. An ambulance with flashing lights had passed him, heading for the hospital. The fire truck still sat at an angle in the parking lot. Firefighters were folding up the hose while one looked into the shattered window of what Sam assumed was the office.

The uniformed police officer who had probably been the first responder—or maybe second, the fire station wasn't far away—saw Sam and relief spread on his face.

"Detective," he said, approaching. "One of the victims is on the way to the hospital, but the woman and child are still here. Two other witnesses stayed, too."

Clearly, this had not been an accident.

"What do you know?" Sam asked.

Not much, it developed. The officer hadn't had a chance to ask many questions. The kid had been hanging on his mother crying, and she'd crawled to hover over the injured man until he was loaded into the ambulance.

Sam glanced toward a woman who sat on the asphalt with her back to the post supporting the gate, her body curled around a small boy, her entire focus on him. She was disheveled, dirty, brown hair falling out of a ponytail. A couple of guys, maybe in their thirties, leaned against a pickup truck that sat askew in the parking lot well away from the concrete block building.

Sam decided to take a look inside before talking to anybody and joined the firefighter in the office.

The mess wasn't quite what he'd expected. Several tall, metal file cabinets had been pulled over. File folders and papers spilled out, but it appeared most had fed a bonfire lit right behind the counter. A charred trail led to the heavy door, now propped open.

The firefighter, a man he knew, glanced at Sam. "Doesn't take a marshal to tell us this was arson."

"No. Whoever set this wasn't subtle." Sam scrubbed a hand over his jaw, feeling some rasp. "Guess I'd better hear the story."

He chose the two guys first.

"Detective McKeige." He pushed his twill shirt back to show the badge attached to his belt. "What can you tell me?"

They exchanged glances. "We were just driving past," one said. "Gene here saw smoke coming out of the building, so we pulled in. The woman pushed open the door. Her kid stumbled down the stairs, and she pulled a guy out. He, uh, didn't look so good. Like he'd had a beating. I saw her stamp out fire that had caught on the leg of his pants. I don't know if he was burned otherwise."

"We piled out and ran. I grabbed the guy. I'm a volunteer firefighter in Sultan," the second guy said. "Slung him over my shoulder and took off while Kenneth helped the woman and kid. We were afraid the windows might blow out or the fire might shoot up through the roof." He shrugged. "Called 9-1-1."

"Did you see anybody else around?"

"Before we saw the smoke, an SUV peeled out of the lot here and headed for the highway. Looked like it was really moving. Too far away for me to tell you make or model, much less license plate. Once sirens sounded, a few people who were picking up or dropping off stuff in their units came running. The fire chief told them to go back to what they were doing but not to try to leave until somebody came to talk to them."

"Okay," Sam said. "Let me get your names and phone numbers."

Both handed him driver's licenses; he snapped pictures of them, jotted down phone numbers, thanked them and let them go.

Then he walked toward the woman, whose head lifted before he reached her. The boy twisted in her arms and stared at Sam, too. Sam ignored the familiar squeeze in his chest that resulted from the look. The boy's hair was about the same color as his mother's, but his eyes were a bright blue, even as reddened and puffy as they were right now.

The woman hadn't cried, but he recognized shock when he saw it. He pegged her as late twenties and pretty. Maybe more than that, under better circumstances. High, curving forehead, great cheekbones, chin on the stubborn side and eyes that were…not blue, like her kid's—assuming this was her child—but light. Gray with a hint of green, maybe.

She started to make getting-up motions, and he shook his head. "You're fine where you are. I'll come down to your level."

An attempt at a smile wavered. "Thank you."

Sam lowered himself to one knee and smiled at the boy. "I'm a police officer. My name is Sam McKeige. What's your name?"

"Toby," he whispered.

"Nice to meet you, Toby. I hope you weren't hurt."

The boy shook his head. "I was fast."

Sam grinned. "Good for you." He transferred his gaze to the woman. "I'm hoping you can tell me what happened here. Nobody else seems to know. I wonder if Toby might like to sit in the fire truck while we're talking."

She kissed the top of the boy's head. "What do you say? Would you like to go look at the fire truck? Maybe climb in?"

His eyes widened. "Can I?"

"The police officer says you can."

Sam waved over the firefighter he'd talked to first, who had no trouble coaxing Toby to accompany him for an up-close-and-personal tour of the rig.

Brave kid.

Watching her son walk away, his hand held by the firefighter, the young woman straightened her back and let out a long breath. Sam thought her teeth chattered toward the end.

"It was...weird," she started.

"First, I'm Detective McKeige. Can I get your name?"

"Oh, I'm sorry. I'm Erin Reed."

"Do you rent a unit here?"

"Not right now. Sometimes I have one for a few days."

She stopped, apparently realized that sounded odd. "I have a booth in the antique mall right off the highway, and I sell on eBay and I've just started a shop on Etsy. Online," she added, although she must realize that was unnecessary. "I buy stuff where I can get it. Garage sales are good, but mostly I buy the contents of storage units being auctioned off because the previous owner quit paying the rent."

Sam vaguely knew that happened and nodded.

She explained that she'd won the auction on a particular unit at this facility a couple of weeks ago. Actually, on three of them, but she was worried because she'd found some quite valuable antique furniture in the one.

"I can't imagine how it ended up abandoned. I'm trying to convince Jeremy—" She paused. "Jeremy Conyers owns this facility. He's on his way to the hospital."

Sam nodded again, watching the subtle, shifting expressions on her fine-boned face. "I wanted to try to contact the previous owners. There may be heirs who, for some reason, didn't realize their parents had stored such amazing stuff. Or... I don't know. I mean, it's mine legally now, but ethically, I'm not so sure. I sold one piece of furniture for a ton of money and then had an attack of guilt."

His eyebrows climbed. How many people wouldn't seize a trove of valuable stuff and run with it, rather than give even passing thought to returning it to someone who didn't know what they'd lost?

"So, you were here to get the name and contact info from this... Jeremy."

"Right, except I've tried before, and he doesn't want to tell me." Her nose wrinkled. "Either that, or the records here are in such a mess, he doesn't know who rented the unit in the first place. His uncle, who owned the facility forever, died a few months ago. You probably noticed the file cabinets. Records are computerized at most storage facilities."

"Ah." Sam wasn't sure what all this had to do with the fire and what might have been an assault on this Jeremy Conyers, but any background was good. He'd never rented a unit at one of these places in his life and kind of wondered why anyone would unless it was just for a month or so during a move.

He stole a glance toward the fire truck, just in time to see Toby being boosted into the cab to sit behind the wheel. Good; he still had time.

"I doubt any of that has anything to do with what happened," Ms. Reed said, but the uncertainty in her voice caught his attention. "I hadn't gotten an answer from Jeremy, but Toby needed to use the bathroom, so I took him. We were just ready to come out when I heard a man yelling at Jeremy. The man wanted to know where his stuff was. He was…hitting and kicking Jeremy. I…saw him swinging a baseball bat at his rib cage." She shuddered. "He kept demanding answers. He wanted names, but I'm not sure why." Her teeth closed on her lower lip, and she looked almost beseechingly at Sam. "One of the names Jeremy gave him was mine."

Chilled, Sam tried to keep his expression from showing his reaction. "We'll ask him why," he said calmly.

She nodded and kept on with the story. The man had gotten angrier and angrier, throwing over the file cabinets, tossing out anything that would burn, starting a fire almost atop Jeremy. A fire that would have killed a stunned man, if she hadn't been there.

She'd had the sense to wait until the assailant fled, then rushed out, deposited her boy at the door, and somehow dragged Jeremy Conyers to the door, out and down three concrete steps. Adrenaline had helped her accomplish the near-impossible. At that point, the two good Samaritans had hustled them all away from danger.

Ms. Reed couldn't give Sam much of a description of the assailant. He'd dressed in black and worn something like a black ski mask over his head and face.

"I think he was pretty good-sized," she said haltingly. "Not as big as you, but... I don't know, maybe six feet? Strong."

Victims always thought their assailants were bigger and more powerfully built than they turned out to be. But in this case, she was a witness, not the victim, which might give her a little more objectivity. He didn't know.

The SUV she'd seen was black, too, but she hadn't taken in the maker, either. "I'm sorry." She looked chagrined. "I just don't pay that much attention to cars unless I'm shopping for one. I should have tried to see the license plate, but—"

"The building was burning down around you, your son and a man who'd just been beaten."

"Well...yes."

Sam smiled and held out his hand. "Think you can get up?"

She seemed to hesitate for a moment before laying her hand in his. Liking the feel of it, slender but strong, Sam glanced down. Her fingernails were clipped short and unpainted. No rings at all, which was interesting.

He rose to his feet, bringing her with him. She was a little taller than average, maybe five foot seven or eight, and what he could see of her curves intrigued him.

He gave himself a mental slap. Her face was streaked

with black, she'd just had a traumatic experience that could have been a lot worse, and he was checking her out as if this encounter was at a bar.

Don't forget the kid, he reminded himself. Even if she was single, even if his scars were as healed as they'd ever be, he wasn't prepared to deal with the boy who was undoubtedly central in Erin Reed's life.

"Do you think the 'stuff' this man was talking about might have been the unexpectedly valuable things that have been worrying you?"

"I…" She flicked a look at Sam as they walked side by side toward the fire truck. "That makes sense, doesn't it?"

"Maybe. It would be ironic considering you've been trying to get in touch."

"Yes. Only… I've won the auctions on the contents of several other storage units in the last couple of months. Three in the past two weeks, a couple of others in the previous month. And it could have been even longer ago that he lost his stuff because of whatever went wrong. So…"

"There's no saying."

"Right. Also, Jeremy gave him at least one other name, too, of someone I know who sells on eBay. He won an auction I was at a couple of weeks ago, and there may have been others."

She was letting him know this wouldn't be simple, Sam concluded. It rarely was, although the tangle of storage facility, valuable antiques and arson as well as a ruthless assailant alarmed him.

"Any chance I can see this furniture you consider valuable?" he asked.

She hesitated. "Yes, although…. I have an awful lot of stuff squeezed in at home. I can't swear what came from that particular lot and what didn't anymore, except for the furniture that stood out."

Her boy came running toward her. Now beaming despite the puffiness that remained around his eyes, he wore a child-size, red plastic firefighter helmet.

"Mommy! Look! I got to almost drive! I want to be a firefighter when I grow up!"

She smoothed his hair with her hand, her smile tender when she looked down at her son. "That's something to think about. We were sure glad to see that fire truck today, weren't we?"

"Uh-*huh*!"

"How come people aren't near as glad to see cops coming?" Sam murmured to her, liking the amusement she didn't try to hide.

"*I* was glad to see you," she said, voice low. "This was scary."

Sam was intrigued to see shyness on her face as she looked away from him.

"It was weird." The bewildered man in the hospital bed didn't look good between the leg in traction, the mummy-like bandages around his head, and the way he gritted his teeth every time he had to take a breath. Looked like he had a couple of burns, too. They glistened from whatever ointment had been supplied, but at least they weren't blistered. His eyes had a glassy look, suggesting he was on heavy-duty drugs.

As for what Jeremy Conyers had said… Wasn't that an exact echo of how Ms. Reed had started?

"Tell me about it." Having pulled a chair up beside the bed, Sam leaned forward, bracing his elbows on his thighs. "Take your time. Let me know if talking hurts too much."

Conyers started to nod, then winced. "Sure. Um. I vaguely noticed someone parking out front, but I was talking to Erin Reed—"

"I've already spoken to her."

He swallowed. "She took her kid off to the bathroom. I guess you know that. But we'd left everything up in the air, so I wasn't paying attention until this man burst in the front door waving a baseball bat. I wanted to shout a warning to her, especially since the boy was with her. But I didn't want to give away the presence of anyone else."

"Smart," Sam said with a nod.

The story offered didn't deviate much from what Erin— Ms. Reed—had told him. The assailant had yelled that he'd learned he'd been locked out of *his* storage unit and his things had been sold at auction, and he wanted to know who had them. The emphasis on *his* was noticeable and undoubtedly mimicry.

The part she hadn't heard was that Conyers asked which unit had been rented to the man. Of course he wouldn't say, since that would have identified him. He'd bellowed something about how the place couldn't get away with stealing many people's possessions, and Jeremy must know who had his things.

"I wish I could have kept my mouth shut," he mumbled. "I *should* have. Only… I thought he was going to kill me."

"You had good reason," Sam said grimly. Seeing Jeremy's increasing distress, either physical or emotional or both, made him feel guilty for pushing, but he had to have answers. "Can you tell me how many names you gave him? And who they are?"

"I think…three or four. He got madder and madder. I

could tell he was losing it." Conyers supplied the names. He looked especially chagrined when he said, "Erin."

"You saved her by not telling your assailant she was there in the building."

His Adam's apple bobbed. "Do you think he'll go after her?"

That was exactly what Sam thought—and feared. He had to ask one more question. "Do you have records of more than those four auctions that have taken place in the, oh say, last six months?"

Jeremy's pained gaze met his again. "They were in one of those filing cabinets. I don't know what survived. And... I'm not even sure who won out on the more recent auctions. It's usually the same half a dozen people bidding. None of them stood out to me."

"We'll hope those records didn't go up in flames."

And, oh yeah, no camera pointed at the parking lot in front.

Chapter Three

Shaken as she was, Erin ditched the idea of going to the antique mall. Instead, she made a rare trip through a McDonald's drive-through and bought lunch for herself and Toby, which they ate at their own kitchen table. It was close enough to nap time when they finished eating that Toby didn't object to going down for his nap—although he begged her to sit with him, which he hadn't done in a long time.

Once he was asleep, Erin called the daycare operator, keeping her voice low.

"I'm afraid it's true that Austin won't be coming here anymore," Mrs. Hall confirmed. "If Toby were here full-time, his mother might have kept bringing him to me, but she felt Austin needed more chances to play with boys his age." She sounded sad, and Erin understood. If you'd taken care of a kid eight hours a day, five days a week, potentially for years, it must be hard to say goodbye.

Erin also heard resignation, meaning Mrs. Hall understood the decision—and expected that Erin might make the same one.

She wouldn't right away. Mrs. Hall was flexible, happy to accept Toby if Erin needed a place to take him out of the blue even if only for an hour or two. But eventually...yes.

Probably.

Although she'd have liked to crawl into bed and pull the covers over her head—or maybe suck on her thumb like she had until she was almost Toby's age—Erin made herself use the time while Toby was sleeping to work. She opened a plastic tub almost at random and found it full of costume jewelry, scarves—a few of them silk—and a collection of purses. Oh, and a pair of knee-high boots and some slippers at the bottom.

Some items she placed immediately in an empty box that would go to the thrift store. The slippers had had it. The boots...maybe thrift store. The scarves smelled musty, but she could wash them. A couple had frayed edges, and she put those in the Toss bag. The silk ones, cleaned and pressed, would sell quickly at her booth in the mall. Sorting the jewelry took most of the afternoon. A few decisions were easy, but she had to get out her jeweler's loupe to look for markings and do Google searches on many pieces. Most also went in the thrift store bag, although she packed them in individual sandwich bags. A few were worth listing online, and she managed photos and even write-ups on them before the doorbell rang.

One box down, a few hundred to go.

Erin had a feeling she knew who she'd find on her doorstep. She wasn't sure whether that feeling was apprehension or something else she didn't want to name.

Sure enough, a peek between blinds showed her that Detective Sam McKeige stood waiting, tall, lean and commanding. And yes, as dauntingly handsome as she remembered. However kind he'd been to her, she had a suspicion that his nature was forceful.

The moment she opened the door, warm brown eyes

studied her. Although, she backtracked on the *warm* part of that description. His gaze was unnervingly sharp and perceptive. He nodded. "Ms. Reed."

"Detective. Come in." Oh, heavens—he'd be appalled by the overwhelming stacks of boxes and more that had devoured so much of her house. She so seldom had people stop by, she tended to forget how abnormal this was. Her cheeks heated.

Of course, his eyebrows rose as he took in the living room and its five-foot-wide path leading to the kitchen. *Hoarder.* That was what he'd be thinking.

"It's…not usually this bad," she heard herself saying. Apologizing. "I've bought too much lately. I've sworn off storage unit auctions until I whittle this down again."

"Uh-huh."

She sighed and led the way to the kitchen, excruciatingly aware of him close behind her. "Let me check on Toby," she said and whisked down the short hall to the bedrooms.

As far as she could tell, Toby was still sound asleep. Thank goodness.

Returning to find the detective standing in the middle of the kitchen, she asked, "Do you have more questions, or do you mostly want to see the furniture?"

"Let's start with the furniture." He cleared his throat. "If you can find it."

She glared at him and was quite sure his mouth twitched into a half smile. She marched straight to the door leading into the garage, knowing it wouldn't look any better organized to him.

Fortunately, she'd grouped the furniture, keeping every piece wrapped in packing blankets. One by one, she pulled the blankets off, let him study the dining room table and set of chairs, the whimsical woodstove, the grandfather clock, the china cabinet the museum curator had agreed was classic Eastlake and finally the wardrobe with flowers inlaid in mahogany.

"Oh, and look at this rocking horse." She uncovered it in turn. "Needless to say, Toby covets it."

McKeige gently set it to moving. His voice softened. "I can imagine."

"I'd let him have it, except it's worth in the neighborhood of two thousand dollars." She turned, finding what she looked for and opening the case. "There's this cello, too. I'll have to get it appraised, since musical instruments aren't my thing, but my best guess is that it'll go for five thousand dollars or more."

"This was a gold mine for you."

"Yes, and there's a ton of smaller stuff, too. The antique tin toys will go like hotcakes online, and I haven't even *looked* in most of the boxes from that unit. Truthfully, I'm not sure anymore that some of the ones from that unit haven't gotten stacked elsewhere. I had a couple of guys empty three units that day and cram the stuff in wherever it fit."

McKeige rubbed his jaw while he looked around. Erin doubted the stubble was a fashion statement, although she could be wrong. It did accentuate a strong jaw and the hollows beneath his cheekbones. She thought she was seeing weariness, as if he was short of sleep.

"I can see why you're worried. You said you already sold a piece?"

She told him the amount it had brought in and who had bought it.

"Museum quality." He eyed the rest of the furniture with a different expression.

"Yes." Feeling chilled, Erin crossed her arms as if to hug herself. "In one way, it's logical to think this is what that man is after. Except…it's all so beautiful, so well chosen. You can imagine what the home looked like where this furniture came from. He doesn't fit."

"No." There was something electric in the detective's eyes when they met hers. "Unless all of this was stolen."

Horrified, she said, "Oh no! I didn't think of that."

"Makes you wonder why he'd quit paying on the unit, though."

"Unless he was in prison?"

McKeige grunted. "But the bills must have been paid up to, what, three or four months ago?"

"Longer ago than that, but yes." She frowned. "Jeremy's uncle hadn't held an auction in quite a while. I think there was no payment for at least six months, from what Jeremy said. Everything in the unit was covered with dust. I'll bet no one had been inside it in years. That doesn't fit with it being a cache of stolen goods."

He let out a long breath. "No, it doesn't. This is a strange one."

"Do you want to see anything else?"

He shook his head and helped her cover everything before scanning the crowded garage again. "Bet you haven't parked in here in a while."

Erin made a face at him. "You'd win that bet."

"Do you own the house?"

"No." Back in the kitchen, she said, "It's a rental. Thank goodness the landlord doesn't bother with inspections."

The low, rough chuckle gave her goose bumps.

She was disconcerted to find herself so attracted to this man. After Shawn had walked out, reminding her that he'd never wanted to have kids—although the unintended pregnancy was no more her fault than it was his—Erin's ability to trust any man had corroded. Even if she scraped the rust away, there might not be anything solid underneath. She couldn't imagine herself having brief hookups, and certainly not while she had a young child at home. Toby was her focus. He had to come first.

And she had no idea why she was thinking about this, anyway. Sam McKeige hadn't given her the slightest indication that he was interested in her that way.

"Would you like a cup of coffee?" she asked.

"I would, if you have time to explain your business more thoroughly."

"Yes, of course." A chair scraped on the floor behind her as she started the coffee maker. Coming back to the table and sitting across from him, she asked, "What do you want to know?"

"Everything." Creases deepened on his forehead. "How long have you been at this? How did you get started?"

Instinctively defensive, she asked, "What does any of that have to do with what happened today?"

"Nothing. I'm…curious. Also, feeling ignorant about the storage unit business, how auctions go and why anyone wants someone's discarded junk."

She could take mild offense at his dismissive tone but chose not to. Instead, she explained how the auctions worked—specifically, that bidders weren't permitted to so much as step inside the unit before they decided what, if anything, they were willing to spend.

He stared at her. "So you're buying blind."

Erin waggled a hand. "Not always. Sometimes furniture, at least, is in plain sight. There are other ways to judge, too. How carefully was the smaller stuff packed? If everything is in cardboard boxes, were they stacked so high the ones on the bottom are getting squished? That suggests the unit doesn't have anything valuable or even breakable in those boxes. Did they buy heavy-duty plastic tubs to make sure nothing got broken? Good sign. But if they bothered to store a sofa that a cat has been using as a scratching post, I tend to think they probably didn't have anything else that's worth my while."

"So you gamble that you'll happen on a unit like the one with the antiques."

"No. I've never hit on anything like this before. I doubt anyone has, at least in this part of the county."

After a moment, Detective MacKeige nodded. Eastern Snohomish County trended toward rural, dotted with small towns mostly strung along the highways. Real money would be in south county, butting up against Seattle and it's prosperous suburbs.

"Do you ever go to auctions in Shoreline, say?"

"No. I doubt I'd ever have the nerve to bid high enough." She told him what she'd paid for the miraculous contents of the one unit. "That's far and away the highest I've ever gone. I just...had a feeling."

"Got it. So, what do you typically find? How do you sell all this?" He nodded toward the dining room visible from his seat at her small table.

With an ear cocked for Toby's reappearance, Erin did her best to give the detective a tutorial of how she sorted and sold the things she found. She showed him the items she'd taken out of the one tub just before he arrived, explaining her decisions, how she determined a value and whether something would be better sold online or in her booth at the mall.

After she poured them coffee, he questioned why she didn't have her own store. She give him a lesson in that, too, including the fact that she'd then have to spend forty hours a week or more there or pay someone else to do it. "And the mall is big enough, with enough variety, to draw people who maybe would think my own store was too small or that the display in the window wasn't exciting. I wouldn't have time to go to storage unit auctions and garage sales—"

"Or you'd be paying someone else to man the cash register."

"Right. Also, I make a lot more with online sales than I do the local ones."

He was interested in that and why she did both. What sold best where? His questions kept coming.

Finally, she asked, "Does this really have anything to do with a guy who was mad because it hadn't occurred to him that the storage unit would get rid of his stuff if he quit paying the rent?"

He gusted a sigh. "Probably not. It's just… What happens when he finds out some of those possessions have already gone into a dumpster or been sold at a thrift store or on eBay?"

That gave her pause. "He'll be even madder?"

"Yeah. And honestly, what you do once you take possession of other people's things probably *isn't* relevant. I just…like to know the context."

"I understand that." She hesitated. "Would you like another cup of coffee? You look tired."

He grimaced, deepening some of the lines in his face,

and ran his fingers through already ruffled brown hair a little darker than hers. "I got called out for what looks like a gang shooting last night that left one guy dead and a woman in critical condition."

"Oh. I suppose you do always have several investigations going at a time."

"'Several' is an understatement. The population in the county has boomed, with a lot of that spilling out of the cities that have their own police forces. We stay busy. Most of those investigations move along slowly, and I concentrate on the latest incidents. In fact, several of us worked last night's shooting, and I'll probably hand off my part in it to focus on today's assault."

Relieved, she bobbed her head. "What do you think will happen next?"

"My gut says this guy isn't going to shrug and say damn, easy come, easy go. There was something in the unit that's important to him."

"That something might be easily recognizable…"

"Or not," he agreed. "Next thing I'll do is warn the other folks Mr. Conyers named. I'd tell you to focus on your more recent acquisitions, except—"

He didn't have to finish. A faint twist of his lips told her what he thought about her jam-packed house.

"It's just Toby and me." That popped out without conscious thought. "We don't need a lot of space. If I stored all this somewhere else, it would eat away at my profits."

McKeige grimaced. "I do see that. If you're really making a living from this—"

"I am. I make more than I would holding any job I qualify for." She pushed back her chair and stood, annoyed that she had to justify her livelihood or any of her decisions. Who was this man to judge her?

The expression on that lean face guarded, he rose to his feet, too. "I apologize if I sounded critical. I didn't intend to. I suppose I always thought those people who hold up the line at the post office are doing the eBay thing part-time."

"Post offices aren't as busy as they used to be. They should be grateful for eBay sellers that use the service."

"They should." Now she'd swear his eyes smiled. "Thank you for your patience." His gaze strayed past her, and he said with unexpected gentleness, "Your future firefighter is awake."

She looked at Toby standing in the door of the kitchen, rubbing his eyes from his nap, then back at McKeige. Was that pain she saw flashing through his eyes? If so, he hid it quickly enough. He clearly didn't intend to linger.

"I need to get moving." He extended a business card to her, undoubtedly identical to the one he'd given her earlier in the day. "I'll be in touch if I learn anything, and you call me if you have any reason to be nervous."

"I will," she agreed, lifted Toby to her hip and led the police officer to the front door. She did not let herself watch as he bounded down the steps and strode toward his unmarked but clearly official SUV. He was an interesting man—okay, sexy—but that didn't have anything to do with her.

Erin just hoped he was good at his job.

JEREMY CONYERS HAD given Sam three names besides Erin Reed's. Sam caught them all at home in the late afternoon. He started with Kevin Hargrove, a thin man who was either balding early or older than Sam's guess of midthirties.

He looked startled when Sam showed his badge but let

him in. They sat in the living room—one *not* being used for storage.

Once Sam described what had taken place today, Hargrove stared at him in horror.

"Erin's okay? And her little boy?"

"Yes. She was quite a heroine. Mr. Conyers likely will be hospitalized for a few days, but the outcome would have been much worse if Ms. Reed hadn't heard what was happening and been able to pull him out."

Hargrove said he'd purchased the contents of only one unit in the past month at that particular storage facility. "Maybe even longer than that," he said. "This is part time for me. I can only go to auctions on my days off." He drove for FedEx, he said, then shrugged. "I keep hoping to get lucky, but, uh, it hasn't happened yet."

Sam listened for resentment or bitterness, but didn't hear either.

"This eBay thing is more a hobby for me than anything," the guy continued.

What about the contents of the unit he'd purchased most recently?

"Nothing to get excited about," he said. "I made the most from a big box of Breyer horses, some of them old enough to be really collectible."

Sam knew what Hargrove was talking about, a pleasant change from the rest of his day. His ex had carted around a box of the plastic horses in hopes she'd someday have a child as horse crazy as she'd been. Michael hadn't seemed especially interested—

Long practice let Sam slam the door on the memory.

"I'll make back what I paid for the contents," Hargrove continued. "Plus a few hundred, I'd say. I can show you what's left. I mean, I took a bunch to two different thrift stores, threw some stuff out. I don't have quite everything up online yet. That's time-consuming."

He had everything laid out on long folding tables in his garage, set up to allow him to park in half of it, Sam couldn't help noticing. Sam didn't see anything he could imagine inciting the previous owner to rage, but he had to issue a warning.

"Problem is," Sam said before leaving, "the man who attacked Mr. Conyers had several names, one of which is yours. He doesn't know which one of you bought the contents of the unit that was previously his." He handed over another business card. "Call 9-1-1 if anything at all makes you uneasy. If you see something—say, someone peering in your windows—call me."

"If my place gets broken into, it'll probably be when I'm at work, don't you think?"

"That would make sense, but this guy's behavior wasn't rational this morning," Sam cautioned.

Hargrove gulped, nodded, thanked him and said, "Maybe I'd better hide the stuff I haven't sold yet."

Sam left that decision up to him, since he was confident the creep wasn't after Breyer horses.

The next two visits weren't as clear-cut. The second was to a fortyish woman whose husband was a long-haul truck driver. She was alone in a rambling house on acreage at least half the time.

Like Erin, Larissa Cavender wasn't quite sure what in her detached garage had come from sales at that particular storage facility. She didn't have the accumulation that Erin did, but there was plenty she hadn't examined yet.

"Haven't found anything out of the ordinary," she said, looking worried. "I wish I had."

He issued the same cautions, more uneasy about Ms. Cavender than he was about Kevin Hargrove or Walt Smith, the other man he'd managed to connect with. She was a woman who didn't work daytimes and was, therefore, usually home.

When Sam quit for the day, he went home even though he had a suspicion the pickings for dinner would be slim. Quiet sounded good to him.

Quiet, he realized shortly after getting home, that would allow him to run the events of the day repeatedly in his head and brood. Sam wasn't surprised that his thoughts turned first to Erin—and to her cute little boy. The kid made her even more vulnerable than she'd be on her own. What good had it done to tell her to watch out?

Even knowing the other eBay sellers were at risk, Sam worried most about Erin. He told himself it wasn't only because she drew him as no other woman had in longer than he could remember. Or because of the little boy who didn't look as much like Michael as Sam had first thought...but there was something there that had triggered an ache beneath his breastbone.

Chapter Four

"Oh, Erin!"

Recognizing the voice, Erin turned once she'd finished buckling Toby into his seat in her pickup truck. "Andrea. Hi."

Her neighbor, half of a nice couple whose youngest child had just graduated from high school leaving them empty nesters, wasn't smiling for once. "I wanted to tell you, last night was Darren's poker night, and he didn't get home until almost one o'clock. I'd long since gone to bed."

Erin tensed, almost certain this wasn't going anywhere good. "You and me both."

"The thing is, somebody was walking around your house, even peeking in windows, or that's what it looked like to Darren, anyway. When the headlights hit this person—Darren thinks a man or maybe a teenage boy—he bolted. Darren backed out of the driveway and followed him to the corner, but once he got that far, he didn't see a soul. He didn't call 9-1-1, because there wasn't much use in getting someone out here, but he didn't like what he saw."

Goose bumps rose on Erin's arms. "No, that's creepy. Please, tell him thank you for chasing this guy off. I'd like to think it was just some teenager…but why *my* house?"

"Well, you do have an awful lot in there," Andrea said kindly.

Embarrassed but trying not to show it, Erin said, "Yes, but wouldn't you think that would put off any average burglar? I mean, what's he going to do, sit down and start opening boxes with me asleep down the hall? Wouldn't he want a house where he can grab the newest iPhone or some other electronics?"

Andrea nodded. "You're right, that would make more sense. Maybe he was peeking in windows at all the houses on the block. And doesn't *that* make me shiver since he could have been looking in my bedroom window."

It made Erin shiver, too, because she had reason to fear this hadn't been the "average" burglar. Not given the horrific assault and fire yesterday.

"Thanks for letting me know," she said, starting around to the driver side of her truck. "I think I'll call the police to tell them what Darren saw, in case there are any break-ins here in the future. Or were in the past," she added.

"That's smart." The cheerful woman smiled, waved at Toby and called, "Have a good day," before returning to the front porch of her rambler.

Erin decided to wait until she'd dropped off Toby at daycare before calling Sam. It wasn't as if he could do anything about a prowler who'd made a clean getaway, but she felt sure he'd want to know. Just in case.

Toby seemed more resigned than excited to be left at Mrs. Hall's, which of course made Erin feel guilty. But she confronted the same problems with changing to a larger daycare: primarily, that many didn't accept drop-ins, certainly not on short notice, or insisted on payment for a minimum number of hours even if she only needed to leave him for two. Still, she reminded herself that the recent windfall meant she didn't have to watch her pennies quite as closely, and Toby really needed time spent with other boys near to his age, but frugality was a habit.

Maybe she'd visit other daycares in town and see what she thought. There was no hurry, right?

No hurry to call the detective, either. She'd wait until she got home later. Surely the prowler wouldn't return to the same house a second night in a row.

She drove to the antique mall and parked beside the back door so she could easily unload. She'd brought a nice floor lamp, several decorative pillows, a handsome bedside stand and several boxes of smaller items that she had no doubt would be quickly snapped up.

She apologized to women browsing her booth when she started stacking boxes in front.

"Ooh, did you bring some goodies?"

She smiled. "I did. Let me finish unloading my truck so I can lock up, and you can check out the new stuff once I've had a chance to set it out."

Two of the three women set aside items they'd already decided to buy, with her promise to hold them until they worked their way back to her space.

She always enjoyed restocking. To her eye, some booths were too thinly stocked. Others were crowded, with dinnerware, jewelry, antique tools and a dozen other miscellaneous things shoved onto shelves together whether they belonged together or not. Erin tried to hold to themed sections: kitchen, garments and accessories, jewelry—mostly in a glass case—books, decorative items and so on, all displayed on furniture that was also for sale. Artwork she fit in as she could.

She'd heard gossip that the space next to hers might be vacant soon. The guy who rented it didn't do a good job of stocking it, and a lot of the stuff he had for sale looked more thrift store than antique store to her. She'd already put in her bid to expand into that space, if and when it did become available. Just think! She might be able to have her dining room back.

At the thought, she cringed a little, remembering the way the detective had studied the piles that filled too much of her house. She hadn't exactly seen contempt on his face but possibly disdain.

She shouldn't let that bother her. Who cared what he thought? But she was afraid she did. She'd had to let him see so much of the reality that made up her life. And no, she wouldn't have been a social butterfly even if her home looked like other people's, but she was self-conscious enough to make excuses to avoid inviting anyone into her home.

Fortunately, she'd priced everything last night, because the three women came back and snapped up a surprising amount before she even found a spot to set it down. They were followed by other customers, and she ended up staying longer than she intended to chat with people, get an idea what they were looking for, even arrange to bring a round oak table she had in the garage for someone to look at the next day. By the time she left, she'd collected a large sum at the front counter.

"You're going great guns!" Marsha Van Beek declared as she signed the check with a flourish and handed it over. "This doesn't even include what you've sold in the past couple of hours. I haven't had time to tally it."

"I know you haven't. There's no rush. And it was a good

day, wasn't it? I'm having a fabulous run on garage sales and storage unit auctions. I could refill my space here every day and hardly have a dent in what I've piled up at home."

"Well, you're definitely my top seller," the owner of the mall said. "I'd love to see you be able to bring in more furniture."

Erin would love that, too. She told Marsha about the couple she planned to meet in the morning, with a promise that the mall would get their cut if they purchased the table.

Marsha, a slender woman with hair of constantly changing color cut in a chic bob, had heard about the fire at the storage facility. She hadn't known Erin had been involved, though, and asked avid questions. Erin was a little bit glad to escape.

She let herself out the back door, where the parked cars belonged to proprietors of the various spaces in the large mall—fifty-eight at last count—as well as Marsha and the clerks who worked what hours Marsha couldn't be here or that were especially busy. This was the first time ever that Erin paused, holding the door with one hand, to study the parked cars and look for movement before she let the door lock behind her.

She didn't like the shiver of apprehension that had her hustling to jump into the cab of her truck and lock *that* door before she even inserted the key in the ignition. She was glad she'd been able to park so close.

The fire itself, and hearing Jeremy share her name with the man beating him, had been bad enough, but picturing some dark-clad man circling her house, peering in windows and probably checking whether doors were locked made it all more real. The monster who attacked Jeremy might come after her.

Would telling Detective McKeige what Darren had seen really do any good? Pulling out of the parking lot and flicking on her signal to turn onto the highway, Erin wondered if he had the power to arrange for a patrol officer to pass regularly down her street.

The town council had decided a couple of years ago that they'd save money by firing their police chief and two officers and contract with the county for law enforcement services instead. Until now, she hadn't had an opinion either way, but she'd heard grumbling from people who claimed getting a response after a crime took longer than it used to, and having a deputy driving through town wasn't the same as having officers stationed right here.

Sam had come quickly yesterday, though. No, she shouldn't think of him by his first name. Detective McKeige had arrived in a timely fashion, not that far behind the firefighters coming from the station half a mile away. He must have been in the area. But why? To interview someone about the night's crime? Were those people locals?

Suddenly aware she'd been driving on autopilot, she glanced at the storage facility as she passed, seeing poor Jeremy's SUV parked outside the blackened office. Was he even out of the hospital? Even if he was, she doubted he was in any shape to drive. She didn't envy him the task of cleaning all that up, and especially not of having to sort salvageable papers to try to restore records. She hoped the computer had survived unscathed. She presumed it held the most current records about renters and their payments. If not…oh, that would be disastrous!

She stuck to the speed limit, which didn't seem to be popular. She winced as the latest passer had to cut sharply into the westbound lane inches from her fender because he hadn't allowed enough room to pass. Did he really think he'd get there that much faster than she did? What was more, the line was a double-yellow. If a cop had seen, he'd have earned an expensive ticket.

A few drivers stayed behind her. She must have noticed them unconsciously, because a stir of unease told her the big black SUV had been there, a couple of cars back, since shortly after she turned onto the two-lane highway.

Unfortunately, black was a popular color with men who liked to drive giant vehicles, from a Tahoe or a Durango to a Ford 250 or a Silverado. Just because this one reminded her on a visceral level of the vehicle at the scene of the fire didn't mean every big black truck belonged to the enraged arsonist.

Even so, she found her gaze flicking to the rearview mirror often after that. When she made a left turn into town, squeezed between the highway and the river, the SUV did, too. She briefly relaxed when she lost sight of it—it must have made a turn. But then she was blocks from Mrs. Hall's house when she saw it behind her again...or one that looked similar.

He couldn't be *following* her, could he? If so, if it was him, was he a danger to the kids at Mrs. Hall's home daycare?

No, that didn't make any sense. But Erin knew she didn't like the idea of that masked man knowing where she left Toby sometimes. Or where she lived. She had only a phone number listed in the skinny local directory, but this wasn't a big town. If somebody had asked for directions...

Erin drove by Mrs. Hall's, turned at the next corner, cut through an alley, and parked in front of a stranger's home. Keeping her eye on her mirrors and windshield, she took out her phone, found the card Detective McKeige gave her and dialed.

SAM STRAIGHTENED IN his chair, lifting his feet from his desk to plant them on the floor. "You think you're being followed?" Disquiet—no, alarm—jolted him. "You say you've pulled to the curb? Do you see the vehicle?"

"No-o. Maybe I'm shying at shadows." Erin Reed sounded timid now. "It's just… I don't know why, but I don't want that crud from yesterday knowing where I leave Toby."

"That's understandable."

"I probably wouldn't have called," she admitted, "except my next-door neighbor told me something this morning."

What she told him redoubled his worry. Yeah, break-ins weren't uncommon in any community. But the odds of someone casing this woman's house within two days of the fire and assault at the storage facility? Sam didn't buy it as chance.

"Okay," he said. "Why don't you go to the daycare now and pick up your boy, as long as you don't see the vehicle again. Was it an SUV or a pickup truck?"

"An SUV," she said, only the faintest of tremors in her voice still betraying her nerves. "I'm sure yesterday's was, too."

"The other two witnesses agree. Put me on speed dial. If you see the SUV again, in the neighborhood, behind you on the road or near your house, call me. I was about to call it a day and leave anyway. I'll stop by and talk to your neighbor, see if he can tell me anything he didn't mention to his wife."

"Thank you," Erin said. "I should tell you it can wait until tomorrow, that you deserve to be able to go home, but—I'm scared."

"You have reason to be." He didn't even look up when a detective he often worked with escorted a shambling man who had to be homeless past his desk. "Staying alert is smart."

She thanked him again and hung up. Sam rolled his shoulders to relieve tension he hadn't realized was building, grabbed everything he needed from his desk and stood to go. This satellite office was located in Monroe, one of the largest cities in east county and home to a huge Washington state correctional institution. A fair number of men Sam had arrested resided there. Seeing the walls of the prison when he went by gave him pause.

He hadn't thought to ask which neighbor—right or left—of Erin Reed's house had been the one to see the prowler. He almost made it an excuse to knock on her door before as well as after talking to the neighbor but didn't let himself. He looked up the address and found a Darren Hillyard right next door to Ms. Reed's rental.

The guy was home and happy to talk. He stepped out on the porch and gestured as he described seeing someone dressed in black, or at least dark colors, coming from the back of her house and stopping to look in a window to the garage.

"Erin keeps a bamboo blind pulled down, so I know he couldn't see anything. I don't know about the slider in back or the bedroom or kitchen windows, but it didn't look good. I'd have called 9-1-1 right then, except my headlights glanced right off him as I turned in, and he broke into a dead run. Took me a minute to back out of my driveway and follow." Darren shook his head. "Could have gotten into a car parked at the curb around the corner, or he might just have been hiding in someone's shrubbery or around back of one of the houses."

"Did you happen to notice what vehicles were parked along the street?"

Darren's forehead creased. "I did. I mean, I was trying to see if anyone was sitting in any of the cars. Most everyone in the neighborhood has a garage or a carport, at least, not to mention the driveway. So it's usually the beater some kid's friend drives that you'll see at the curb." He was thinking hard, showing a hint of perplexity.

Sam didn't say a word to interrupt the cogitation.

"There was a big SUV midway down the block. Right before the alley that passes behind Erin's house and mine. Not a crossover." He shook his head. "Wish I knew my cars better."

"What color was it?"

"I want to say black, but there isn't a streetlight right there, so it could have been, I don't know, dark blue or something like that."

Sam pulled up images of full-size SUVs on his phone and gave Darren plenty of time to scroll through. He ruled a few out and thought what he'd seen was angular, not as rounded and modern as a few of the newest models. But he ended up shaking his head again.

"Could be a Yukon, Suburban, Expedition… I'm sorry. I wish I could be more help."

"You were observant," Sam told him. "I suspect the prowler jumped into his SUV and lay down across the seats, something like that. No reason you'd have gotten out and shone a flashlight in." Seeing Darren's expression, Sam added, "If a situation like this arises again, please *don't* do anything like that. Hang back and call 9-1-1. Or me, if it involves Ms. Reed's house or what appears to be that same vehicle."

They walked back together, and Sam gave him a card with his mobile number on it. Thanking him again, Sam jogged up to Erin's small porch to ring the bell. He wished he could reassure her instead of further frightening her.

AFTER THE DOORBELL RANG, feet thundered through the living room. Fortunately, although Toby could reach the doorknob, the dead bolt was too high.

"Wait up!" she called anyway, following to find him bouncing up and down in impatience. What a surprise—he wore his fireman's hat. He was barely willing to take it off to go to bed.

"It's the 'tective," he declared. "Isn't it, Mom?"

"I don't know who it is." She used the peephole to assure herself that, yes, Detective McKeige was on her doorstep, as tall and daunting as always.

But on my side, she reminded herself, *so why daunting?* She knew, though; his presence threatened her belief she neither needed nor wanted a man in her life. Right now, she did need him.

"Guess what?" she told her eager son. "You're right! It is Detective McKeige." She unlocked the dead bolt, then smiled at Toby. "Do you want to let him in?"

"Uh-huh!" Turning the doorknob was a two-handed job for him, but he succeeded, tripping and hanging from the knob as he pulled the door open. "Hi! Mommy said *I* could let you in."

The detective smiled, although once again she saw a flicker of something in his eyes. Discomfort? "Thank you. Still planning to become a firefighter, are you?"

"Yes! I liked driving that big red truck."

McKeige laughed. "I thought about becoming a firefighter instead of a police officer, but this suits me more. You may find you're interested in all kinds of jobs before you get old enough to decide."

"What kind of jobs?"

"Oh, I wanted to be an astronaut or a rancher… I have horses and enjoy riding—"

"Uh-oh," Erin mumbled.

McKeige's sharp gaze flicked to her. "That's on his list?"

Toby's blue eyes widened. "You have a horse? Of your *own*?"

"I do. Maybe someday you can, too."

"Can I—?"

Erin cut him off. "We don't ask for favors. Detective McKeige is here to talk to me about the fire and the scary man. We need to let him do that."

Toby reluctantly shuffled back and let McKeige in.

"Why don't we talk in the kitchen?" Erin said. "Toby, you can go back to playing."

His voice rose to a whine. "Can't I…?"

She raised her eyebrows.

He sagged, looked reproachful and trudged down the hall toward his room.

The detective grinned. "You should add 'actor' to his list."

She laughed. "You're right."

He followed her through the stacks of boxes and furniture without comment, agreed he wouldn't mind a cup of coffee and sat at her kitchen table.

"He's a great kid," he said, with restraint.

"Yes, he is." She took mugs from the cupboard, glad coffee was already brewing. She wanted to ask if he had children, but something held her back. Maybe he did have a son, but didn't see him often after a divorce. That would explain what she thought might be pain when he looked at Toby.

They weren't friends. She couldn't expect him to tell her something like that. No, he wanted to talk about a violent, masked man who likely had been looking in her windows last night while she and Toby slept.

Apprehension tightened her throat. "Did you find out anything?"

Chapter Five

Nothing Detective McKeige told her surprised Erin. Instead, her anxiety climbed into the red zone. This was ridiculous. She'd lived a quiet life, her divorce the greatest drama in it—and divorce was an all-too-common drama.

"Why me?" she heard herself say and knew she sounded piteous. She shook her head before he could answer. "I know, I know. It's because Jeremy gave this guy my name. But why wouldn't he tell Jeremy what he's so desperate to get back? Most of us would probably give it to him without even charging him, and at most we'd expect to be reimbursed for what we paid at the auction."

"Which I gather in most cases wouldn't be any more than the several months of payments he must have missed."

"Less!" She wrinkled her nose. "Expect for the big unit full of the exceptional stuff. And even that…"

He offered a crooked smile. "You've been *trying* to find the owners so you can give it all back."

"Well…some of it." At a tilt of his eyebrows, she sighed. "I've already earned way more than I paid for the contents just from the one sale."

"Do you have any idea how rarely I encounter a person who is so determined to do the right thing?"

"I can't be *that* unusual."

"Maybe not." He stretched his arms over his head until she heard cracking sounds, groaned and then dropped them to his sides. "I'll admit, in my line of work I don't often meet the cream of society."

"Unless they're victims," she said ruefully.

His smile might have made her blush. She hoped not.

Before either could say anything else, his phone rang. He took it out, frowned and answered, "Detective McKeige."

All Erin heard was a man on the other end of the call talking quickly.

"Okay," McKeige said, "I'm on my way." He ended the call. "That was Kevin Hargrove. I gather you know him? He came home from work to find the contents of his garage trashed."

"Oh no!" Kevin didn't make an awful lot from his efforts. Erin hoped this didn't discourage him from continuing to try. She'd started with the auctions and garage sales as a way to support herself and Toby without having to put Toby into daycare for long, expensive hours. But she'd discovered what she did was fun, too, and she'd hate to see someone like Kevin give up. Everyone needed to have a dream. "At least he wasn't home."

"That's something," the detective agreed, pushing back his chair.

"I forgot to pour the coffee," she realized.

He chuckled. "I'm fine. I've been mainlining it all day. Before I go, did you have any questions?"

"Is there anything I should do that I'm not already?"

Creases formed on his forehead. "You did put me on speed dial?"

She nodded.

"Let me repeat—if anything at all doesn't seem right,

call 9-1-1 and me. Don't hesitate." Muscles flexed in his jaw. "I wish…" A slight shake of his head told her he'd cut himself off. "I'll be in touch."

Her head bobbed, and she followed him to the front door. "Tell Kevin I'm sorry this happened."

"I'll do that." McKeige opened the door and turned to look at her, gaze troubled. "I'm worried about you most of all. You and Toby—" Again he stopped himself. "Reality is, you have the most stuff here. The others are hobbyists in comparison. He may quickly dismiss other names on the list. If this guy realizes how much you have crammed in here, he's going to focus on *you*."

She took an involuntary step back. "But…somebody Jeremy didn't even name could have bought the contents of the unit. I mean, does this guy even know *when* his stuff was sold?"

"That's a good question, and I'll be asking Mr. Conyers. Has he taken a call in the recent past from someone who realized they'd dropped paying for whatever reason? You'd think he would remember, unless it happens too often."

"At the bigger facilities, there usually are several units a month." Although some people just quit bothering to pay because their stuff wasn't that valuable. Even people who couldn't keep up payments normally wouldn't go off the deep end this way. "But Jeremy only inherited something like three months ago. Before that…" She shrugged.

"Yeah." McKeige's frown deepened. "You be careful, Erin."

Were they on a first-name basis now? Or did that go only one way? And what a frivolous thing was that to be thinking about, given the frightening knowledge that she

likely did have whatever this nutcase was after...and that
he didn't hesitate to hurt anyone who got in his way.

How was she supposed to figure out what he *was* looking for?

WITH THE DOOR left up, afternoon light supplemented the
lone bulb overhead in Kevin Hargrove's garage. Was this
a major crime? No, but Sam was appalled nonetheless. The
rage demonstrated here equaled what he'd seen at the storage facility—there just hadn't been a human being for the
intruder to vent his fury on.

Everything so carefully set out on folding tables had
been swept to the concrete floor. At a guess, booted feet
had trampled on all of it, crushing the breakables. An ax
that had presumably hung on the wall with other tools had
been used to smash even the tables. The single window was
shattered. The ax had been left embedded in a workbench
built-in beneath it.

If Hargrove had been home, he'd be dead.

Sam breathed a word he shouldn't have said under his
breath. He glanced to see Hargrove staring with shock, even
though this wasn't his first sight of the mess.

"Did you touch anything?" Sam asked.

The guy shook his head.

"I'm going to ask you to leave it all as-is behind a closed
garage door until I can get a technician out here, probably
tomorrow, to dust for fingerprints and search for anything
the intruder may have left behind."

Hargrove's head turned slowly, his eyes dazed. "Nothing here was worth that much."

"No, but this has to be the man who battered Jeremy
Conyers and set the office on fire, likely hoping he'd die

in the fire. He's going to visit everyone else on his list, and my worry is that one of those people will be at home." Larissa Cavender. Erin Reed, made even more vulnerable by her young son. "I'm giving this my all, and I'm including the damage to your property."

Hargrove's prominent Adam's apple bobbed. "Thank you."

Sam retreated from the garage, and the homeowner pushed a button on the remote he clutched to let the door clatter down.

"I was talking to Ms. Reed when you called," Sam remembered to say. "She was upset that this happened to you and doesn't want this to discourage you from pursuing the storage facility auctions." Had she said that? He didn't know but felt sure that was what she'd meant.

Hargrove tried to smile. "If you see her, tell her thanks. I'd a hundred times rather this—" he paused, struggling with what to call the offender "—monster came here than her house. She's a nice lady, and she has that cute kid. Have you met him?"

"Yes." Sam shared Hargrove's horror. "I've encouraged her to call for help if she hears so much as a creak that doesn't sound normal." He didn't say that he suspected he wouldn't be sleeping well during the nights to come, not when he expected that call from her.

He filled out a quick report for Hargrove to give his insurance company and left, not as glad to be heading home as he should be. He'd intended to cook instead of grabbing takeout but figured he had to have a microwaveable meal in his freezer. He'd lost enthusiasm for the rerun of a Seahawks game he'd missed because of work, too. Honestly, he was tempted to drive back to Erin Reed's neighborhood, park down the street and keep an eye on her house.

Overkill, he told himself and took the turn onto the highway that would lead him east toward Monroe and the old farmhouse he owned on some acreage on the outskirts.

He knew what Toby had wanted to ask him. Even if putting the kid up on one of his horses would bring back memories he tried to block, he should offer.

The turn signal clicked as he grimaced. With luck, they'd stop this scumbag before Sam had to see the hope on Toby's face again.

THE NEXT MORNING, Erin winced at the sight of herself in the mirror. Her eyes looked sunken, and the dark circles below didn't help. That was what sleeplessness did for you.

She mostly planned to work at home, although she'd intended to grocery shop. Forget that. She could scrounge up meals of some kind. Toby would be happy if she fed him grilled cheese sandwiches for lunch and macaroni and cheese for dinner. They'd manage.

Unfortunately, she had promised to haul that round oak table to the antique mall to show it to the couple. She should put on some makeup so she didn't look like one of the walking dead, but that seemed like too much effort.

The couple were delighted by the table, which they claimed was exactly what they wanted to fit in a nook in an old house they'd recently bought. They shifted the item to the back of their truck, and she and Toby walked them in so they could pay for it through the clerk behind the counter. Then she hoisted Toby onto her hip and fled without even checking her booth.

As the day went on, she wished she'd taken Toby to Mrs.

Hall's for a few hours. He tried, he really did, but couldn't entertain himself for an entire day while she worked. They kicked a ball out in the backyard for a while, with her making a mental note that she needed to mow, and she played several games with him. Thank goodness he still napped.

She set up to take photos of some of the things she planned to list on eBay or Etsy, a finicky process that required concentration. Those photos had to be crystal clear, appealing…and honest.

Dinner… Well, she'd load up on veggies tomorrow. And just about everything else. She had enough milk for the mac and cheese out of a box, margarine was getting low, and Toby would have to settle for a frozen waffle tomorrow, since no milk meant no cereal.

Her phone hardly rang all day. She called the hospital and learned Jeremy had been released, but he didn't answer his cell phone. Tomorrow would do. He was probably sleeping, the way she wished *she* were.

Detective McKeige neither called nor stopped by. The man presumably had investigations that didn't involve her. As long as nothing happened…

After putting Toby to bed that evening, Erin sat down to pay bills. She gave up after she tried to add an extra thousand dollars onto her rent and was able to delete a few numbers before it was too late.

Tomorrow, she thought for at least the twentieth time today. She was too tired to do anything *but* sleep tonight.

Of course, she checked locks on doors and windows several times. She also picked up a soundly sleeping Toby and carried him into her room to sleep with her, something she rarely allowed. Finally, she set a low stool and one of

Toby's toys out in the hall. Hopefully, they would trip anyone who tried to creep in the dark toward their bedrooms.

Feeling like that was the best she could do, she brushed her teeth, crawled into bed and was out as fast as her bedside lamp.

SHE STARTLED AWAKE. What…? Belatedly, Erin realized Toby was in bed with her. Had he kicked her or—? But then she heard a sound she couldn't identify. It wasn't loud, but it didn't *belong*.

She lay there stiffly and strained to listen. Had the sound been here in the house, or was she just hearing something outside? A cat jumping over the fence, making the gate rattle?

A thump came next, quiet enough it might not have awakened her in the first place, and she knew: it was out in the garage.

If anything at all doesn't seem right, call 9-1-1 and me. Don't hesitate.

There'd been enough intensity in Sam's husky voice that Erin groped for her phone on her bedside stand. Her hand shook.

9-1-1 first. Would somebody in the garage be able to hear her? She didn't think so, not if she kept her voice low.

Never mind, she'd call Sam first. She wouldn't have to explain to him. He could call 9-1-1 for her.

His phone rang three times before he came on, sounding wide-awake. "Erin?"

"I think somebody is in the garage. I… Will you call 9-1-1 for me?"

"Yes, and I'm on my way. Don't go out there."

Her breath caught at a scraping sound. The door from

the garage into the house was steel. Had some kind of lock-pick skated over the door?

Oh God, oh God.

Toby still slept. She sometimes thought he'd sleep through an earthquake. Right now, she could only be grateful. Keeping him quiet might have been impossible.

Still clutching the phone, she slid out of bed and tiptoed into the hall. Sam was saying something, but she didn't try to make it out. Another scratching sound came to her. Her heart beat so hard, it throbbed in her throat as well as her chest. Her breath came short. She barely remembered in time to dodge the obstacles she'd set out herself. What if she'd gone crashing down?

In the doorway to the kitchen, she stopped. The dim light from the window showed that the door into the garage was still closed. Standing still, she waited.

Then the door seemed to quiver, and a low growl sounded like a profanity, or worse, to her.

She yelled, "I've called the police! They'll be here any minute! And I have a gun, so don't even *think* about trying to come into the house!"

For a moment, nothing happened. Then another curse, and a few thumps rang out. Was that the sound of the side door from the garage? What if the intruder ran by the kitchen window? Erin stepped into the hall.

Finally, she pressed her forehead to the wall and lifted the phone. "Sam?"

No one was there. With her tight clutch, she'd probably ended the call herself.

She stayed where she was, shaking and straining to hear any tiny sound. Had he really fled? And…what would she find in the garage? That was her livelihood out there! What if too much was smashed? And God help her, why had he wanted to come into the house when the garage was stuffed full? The chances were best that whatever this man was determined to find, it was out there.

She couldn't hear the highway from here but did hear a few cars. One maybe a block or two away? And then a siren, distant but gaining in volume rapidly. She hoped with all her being that it was coming here. Probably a patrol officer sent by Sam.

Erin wished it would be him. He made her feel safe, even if she really wasn't. She drew in and let out a shuddery breath. Safe wasn't all she felt when she was with Detective McKeige. He was the sexiest man she'd ever met. More than that, he was large, strongly built, reassuring…and kind.

Flashing lights and a screaming siren were right outside now, probably in her driveway. The whole neighborhood would be awakened. She hurried to the front door to see Sam leaping out of the same SUV he'd driven earlier. He'd turned off the siren but left on the flashing lights. He jogged toward the porch, where she belatedly turned on the light.

His eyes locked on her. "You're all right." His voice was rougher than she remembered.

Hugging herself, she nodded. "I think he's gone."

"Let me circle the house before I come in. Lock the door behind me. Don't open it until I come back."

"Yes. Okay." She did as he asked, becoming aware of another approaching siren.

Just as the next police car pulled to the curb, also cutting off its siren, a rap came on the front door.

She unlocked it, and Sam stepped over the threshold. To her astonishment, he wrapped her in his arms and gave her a hard hug. He didn't let it last long, but he muttered, "You scared me."

Was he supposed to do that? Who cared? She just wanted to stay in the circle of his arms, lay her head against that broad, solid chest. She wanted—

Too much. This was no time for fantasies.

"Detective McKeige?" The voice came from out front. "That you?"

"It's me," McKeige said, still within touching distance. "Looks like the intruder broke in the side door to the garage. I haven't gone out there yet to see what damage has been done. He didn't get in the house?"

At the faint question, she shook her head. "I yelled at him. Said the police were on the way, and I had a gun."

He cocked an eyebrow. "Do you?"

"No." Erin smiled weakly. "Unless there's one in some box I haven't opened yet."

"You might have a whole arsenal out there. Maybe that's what he's mad about. You don't take a man's guns."

"I hope that's facetious."

Under the circumstances, the flash of his grin startled her. "Of course it is." He nudged her backward and made room for the uniformed deputy who stopped on the porch.

"Did you hear a car start, ma'am?"

"I thought I heard one about a block away. The timing would have been about right."

"And how long ago was that?"

"I...don't know." Time felt weird right now. "Um, five minutes? It was before I heard the first siren."

"He'll be long gone then."

Of course. She remembered her one glimpse of the SUV

almost rocking onto two wheels as it turned out of the storage facility.

"Please, come in," she said.

"Where's Toby?" Sam asked.

"Still asleep. Well, I'd better take a quick peek."

The two men followed her through the path between boxes and furniture but presumably stopped to talk. She should be embarrassed anew by the hoarder-house look, but she felt too much to allow it entry now.

The small lump under the covers in her bed hadn't moved at all. She stepped closer and whispered, "Toby?" When there was no response, she laid a gentle hand on his back and felt it moving in the natural rhythm of sleep.

When she eased back into the hall, Sam—oh no, she would use his name talking to him if she didn't quit thinking of him that way—was waiting right outside the door.

"He really hasn't woken up?" he murmured.

"Nope. Thank heavens," she added.

"All right." He backed away. "You'd better come with us. You'll have a better idea than we will what damage has been done or if anything seems to be missing."

"Why would he have been trying to get in the house if he found what he's looking for?"

Somebody had turned on the kitchen light, letting her see the sharp attention from the officer. "He tried to get in?"

Her head bobbed. "I think so. I heard scraping on the door. It's steel, you know. It was metal against metal."

"Son of a—" The detective abandoned her in favor of the door. "You have a dead bolt on it."

"Yes, it was already there. I thought it was kind of unusual, but those push-button ones aren't much use."

"No, they aren't, and the typical cheap wood door can be kicked in, no matter what lock secures it."

"I'll have to thank my landlord."

Sam pulled a pair of thin plastic gloves from a pocket, donned them and undid the dead bolt, then opened the door.

Seeing darkness, Erin said, "The light switch is to your right."

He reached, and light flooded the garage.

The first words out of her mouth were, "Oh no."

Chapter Six

It didn't look as bad out here as he'd expected after hearing Erin's exclamation. He wondered if a whole lot more damage would have been done if the intruder hadn't been trying to keep quiet. Boxes and rubber tubs had been tossed, their contents jumbled, one tub broken beneath the mark of a boot print.

Erin exclaimed and rushed into the garage. Picking up an embroidered shawl, she draped it on a box, then reached for a broken lamp with a fancy porcelain base.

Sam felt a chill as he took in the overall scene and thought he knew what that SOB had been thinking. He'd yanked out boxes looking for his own. Were they cardboard or plastic? If plastic, had he been looking for a particular color? This guy had to be short of patience, which didn't come as a surprise. As long as he stayed quiet, he could have taken hours to search out here. Instead, frustration had seized him, and he'd decided that Erin would *tell* him the location of what he wanted.

Sam's initial fear for her had settled once he saw her alive and well. Now it became jagged again. She wouldn't be safe until this creep was behind bars—or dead. He wasn't the giving-up type.

She kept fluttering around, picking things up, then setting them down. He doubted she'd rest easy until she'd re-stored order out here.

"At least we know one thing," he said.

Her head turned. "What's that?"

"He's probably not after the pricey furniture and boxes from the storage unit you paid so much for."

"How can you—?" But she broke off as she looked around. "You're right. He could have seen some of the furniture. And the rocking horse."

"Exactly."

"The only thing is, I don't know if everything that came from that unit is together out here."

Sam almost groaned. Of course it couldn't be that simple.

Deputy Warren, who had stayed silent until now, spoke up. "Can you tell if anything is missing, ma'am?"

She made a funny sound. "No. How could I? I mean, he could have pocketed some small things from one of the boxes he opened, but…"

"It's not likely he bothered," Sam said.

"No."

"Come on inside," Sam suggested. "I'll walk Deputy Warren out, then come back. We'll want to secure that out-side door for the night."

"Oh! Yes. I hadn't even thought of that."

They could push a few heavy boxes against the door. Sam didn't say so, but that would work. The door itself was flimsier than the one leading into the house and would need to be replaced.

She set down the couple of things she was holding as if they were incredibly valuable, then walked toward him.

This was a bad time for him to react to her fine-boned,

curvaceous body and tumble of shiny hair. Or maybe he should wonder why he hadn't sooner, given that she wore only a pair of boxer shorts and a snug-fitting tank top. Her breasts swayed when she moved, and he swore he saw the rise of her nipples. Some color rose in her cheeks, and her eyes shied from his. She could probably read his mind.

He backed up clumsily, grateful when the deputy got out of his way. He hoped he was blocking Warren's view of her. She flicked off the light in the garage and slipped by him, letting him pull the door shut.

"I want to talk to you before you go back to bed," he told her, then walked the deputy out.

"I'll file a report," Warren said, pausing on the door-step, "but I get the feeling there's more to this than just tonight's break-in."

Standing on the porch, Sam summarized what had happened so far. The deputy knew about the storage facility attack and arson, of course, but he hadn't been aware of the relatively minor yet still ominous break-in at Hargrove's place.

"This guy will be back," Warren said, frowning.

"Oh, yeah." Sam rolled his shoulders. "I doubt if he'll take the chance of making a return visit tonight, but I'm going to stay anyway. Ms. Reed has a three-year-old son. If this piece of—" He swallowed the rest of it. "If he gets his hands on the boy, she'd do anything."

"I have a boy about that age myself. I would, too."

So would Sam, who'd have sacrificed anything including his life to save Michael. The jab of pain was duller than it had once been, but still hurt.

They said good-night, and Sam went back inside, locked the door behind himself and returned to the kitchen, where he found Erin sitting at the table. Her back was straight, her gaze fixed on the wall in front of her, her hands clasped on the tabletop in front of her. She was too still.

"Okay," he said, staying on his feet. "I'm going to see what I can do about that door. There's no reason you can't get some more sleep, even though I know that seems unlikely right now."

He hadn't seen her blink in so long, her eyes must be dry, but she did turn her head to look at him.

"You're kidding, right? I won't be able to fall asleep. I'd get started out in the garage, except I'd be too far from Toby."

"With your permission, I'll stay so you *can* sleep," he said, making sure there was no give in his voice. "If I can find my way to your sofa—"

Her face crumpled momentarily before she regained control. "That's asking a lot of you, but...you can sleep in Toby's bed. It's a twin, too small for you, but better than the couch. He doesn't usually sleep with me, but tonight—"

She wanted him close. Sam understood.

"A twin bed is fine," he said gently. "I never sleep deeply. Nobody will get into this house without me knowing."

The sudden sheen of tears in her beautiful eyes tempted him to reach for her, but he didn't dare. He was a cop; she needed him. Later, maybe he could give her a call...if he could get past knowing he wouldn't be able to avoid her boy.

"Thank you," she whispered. "You probably have a family but—"

"No family." If he sounded harsh, he couldn't help it.

"I'm sorry. I mean, it's none of my business. I shouldn't have asked."

She hadn't really. He had no business being sensitive.

She'd presumably either gone through a divorce or lost her husband to an accident or illness.

"No, it's okay," he said, quietly. "My wife and son died. It's been a while, but—"

A small hand rested briefly on his arm. "I'm really sorry. Make yourself comfortable. If you want coffee or a bite to eat—"

Immensely relieved she hadn't asked any questions, he said, "No. Once I take care of that door, I'll try to get to sleep, too."

For a lot of reasons, he doubted that would happen.

FEELING ASTONISHINGLY RESTED considering, Erin made it all the way through her morning routine in the bathroom and was in the kitchen before she realized... Toby hadn't joined her yet. Uh-oh.

She rushed down the hall. Toby's bedroom door was open, of course. Still in his pajamas, he stood next to the bed staring open-mouthed at the man who lay on his back, hands clasped behind his head, smiling at her son.

"I borrowed your bed," Sam was saying.

"How come?"

Sam's gaze shifted briefly to Erin, frozen in the doorway, before he said, "Your mom had some excitement in the middle of the night. After that, it seemed like I'd get more sleep here than if I went home." He paused. "She can tell you about it later."

"I'm sorry if we woke you up—" Erin began, but he shook his head.

"Just waiting until you were all done in the bathroom."

"Oh. Um." He had slept in the T-shirt he'd worn beneath a jacket last night, thank goodness, because he'd pushed the covers down to just above his waist. She'd have seen that muscular chest and powerful shoulders bare otherwise. Probably best not to have the picture stuck in her mind.

"Toby, come help me with breakfast," she said. "You'll let me feed you, won't you?" she asked Sam.

"I'd appreciate it. I settle for cereal most mornings."

"Well, we're having waffles from scratch today." They'd have settled for frozen if not for him.

Toby joined her in the kitchen, his expression eager. "What are we gonna do today? Maybe Mr. 'tec...tective can go with us?"

Oh, heavens. It was Saturday, and she'd been thinking they ought to do something fun for Toby, at least for part of the day. Unfortunately, she'd have to call her landlord and hope he didn't want to come out and inspect the damage. Still, Toby came first.

Maybe just lunch, somewhere with bouncy balls... The Evergreen State Fair was going on in Monroe, but it was expensive and really too overwhelming for a child Toby's age. Except money wasn't as tight, she reminded herself, and undoubtedly there would be rides for young children. They could pet some animals, too.

Of course, the ten days of the state fair meant big business at the antique mall, too, as people driving by the sign let themselves be tempted coming or going. Which meant she ought to spend some extra hours there.

"Let me think about it," she said and measured flour into a big bowl.

"Think about what?" Sam asked as he strolled into the kitchen.

She liked the dishevelment of his hair and even the stubble on his jaw. "Oh, we're just making plans for the day."

"Mommy said we could do something fun, but I don't know what," Toby contributed. "Sometimes we take a picnic to the park on the river, an' that's all."

"Hey!" she protested. "You like splashing in the water."

"Yeah, but *today* I wanna—"

"The you-know-what has started," Sam pointed out.

Toby's forehead crinkled, and he opened his mouth to ask questions.

She leveled a look at him. "I said I'd think about it."

Her unexpected guest chuckled. "Can I do anything?"

"The coffee is ready. You can pour yourself some."

He came close enough for his arm to brush her shoulder as he chose one of the mugs she'd set out. She'd put milk on the table—who really kept cream around?—as well as the sugar bowl. He sat down, ignoring both, and took a first sip.

Toby climbed up in his usual place, with the booster seat raising him to an acceptable height. "What are *you* gonna do today?" he asked.

"Probably work for a few hours, then clean my house, maybe?" He frowned thoughtfully, as if considering everything he had to do about her garage break-in.

Toby scrunched his nose. "That's not fun."

"No, it isn't," Sam said apologetically.

Erin added a fourth enormous waffle to the plate she'd kept warm in the oven, then carried it to the table. She wished she had real butter to offer and more than one choice of syrup, but her grocery shopping was strictly limited by the tastes of a preschooler.

As soon as she said, "Help yourself," Sam shifted one of the waffles to his plate, his expression anticipatory. He didn't look picky. She cut a quarter of one of the other waffles for Toby, added margarine and sat down with the rest

of that waffle. She probably should have stopped at three.
She hardly remembered how much Shawn ate, and anyway
he was both thinner and a few inches shorter than Sam.

Toby did most of the talking, his eagerness greater than
his appetite. The landlord definitely would have to wait;
the hope on her son's face always got to her.

Sam had been watching him, too, even as he was on his
second waffle and not yet slowing down. She thought he
sighed when he set his fork down on his plate. "As for the
something fun, I have two suggestions," he said. "One is
the you-know-what. The other is, uh, you two come out to
my place. Toby could get up on one of my horses."

Toby stared at him as if he were the Wizard of Oz. Erin
felt almost as stunned.

"You mean that?" Toby asked.

A muscle jumped in Sam's jaw. "I wouldn't have said it
if I didn't." He resumed eating, but he kept an eye on her
and Toby.

"Mommy?"

"I... That sounds fun to me, too," she heard herself say,
only a little breathlessly. Maybe Sam wasn't thinking of
her as Ms. Reed any more than she thought of him as Detective McKeige.

He smiled, if wryly. "It's settled."

WHAT HAD HE been thinking? Sam watched Toby explode
from the back seat with no help from his mom. What he
should be doing today was checking up on the other auction buyers, talking to Jeremy Conyers again and sticking
with Erin to ensure her landlord bought a steel door with a
dead bolt to replace the one that had been ruined last night.

Had it occurred to her yet that if her landlord came by

to replace the door he'd take a look in the garage and potentially into the rest of the house, too? Not that she was damaging the house…

"You called your landlord yet?" he asked Erin.

She moaned. "No. I'll do it as soon as I get home. I promised Toby a fun day, and… I'm a coward."

"Tell you what," he said. "I'd be glad to replace the door if he'll pay for it."

"You mean, so he doesn't come to the house at all? You're already doing so much…" But she desperately wanted him to do the one more thing, he could tell.

"I don't mind," he said. "I'm going to be keeping a close eye on you and your place anyway."

How close, he wasn't telling her.

If he didn't insist on being brutally honest with himself, he could use the need to watch over her and Toby as an excuse for inviting them to his place today. Of course, that wasn't it. He was pretty sure he'd succumbed to the expression of dawning hope on Toby's face, the one that had triggered an electric shock to Sam's heart. No, Toby didn't look *that* much like Michael, but there was something.

And then there'd been the temptation to spend time with Erin when she was actually happy.

Toby's eyes widened when he saw the two horses waiting at the paddock fence. "Do they have names?" he asked in a hushed voice.

Sam glanced down at the boy. "Nebula is the gray gelding. Daffy is the palomino."

"For Daffodil?" Erin asked.

He grimaced. "Yeah. They came with their names. I just can't quite spit that one out."

She giggled, a sound that he felt like a touch. Damn it.

"They're *big*!" Toby gazed up at the horses with awe.

"He's only been on a pony before, at another boy's birthday party," Erin murmured. "He's been talking about it ever since."

"I can *really* ride?"

"You really can."

Once Sam had learned that Erin grew up riding, although she hadn't been on a horse for several years, he'd decided to saddle both and take them for a short trail ride. That is, unless Toby freaked out to find out how high off the ground he'd be.

Erin had brought a carrot, and Sam left her showing her son how to safely offer treats to a horse. He carried out bridles, saddles and saddle blankets, and demonstrated for his small and rapt audience how to saddle a horse. Toby thought Sam was being mean when he whacked each horse's side while tightening the girth, and Sam had to explain why he did it.

Erin suggested he take Toby up in front of him and ride around the corral behind the barns.

Once Sam swung himself onto Daffy's back, Erin lifted Toby up to him. The kid was warm and wriggly and felt fragile, and for a sharp instant Sam wished he'd never suggested this. It took him back to a place he didn't want to be, but he knew how to don a mask and did. Toby wouldn't notice his tension, but Erin might.

She led Nebula to the corral and used the fence rail there to get a leg over the gelding's back. As Sam held Daffy to an amble around the corral, he kept an eye on Erin until he was sure she knew what she was doing.

Toby was quiet for the first few rounds, and then he said, "Can I hold the reins?"

Sam guided him, showing him how to position his hands, and then let him have the reins. Not that the palomino noticed. She continued to circle without needing guidance, but Toby was delighted.

"I want to gallop!" he declared, bouncing.

"Not today," Sam told him but couldn't hold back a grin. "Shall we go out on a trail?" he asked Erin.

When she agreed, he unlatched the gate from horseback, took charge of the reins again and urged the mare to stretch her legs into a slightly faster walk.

When he turned his head, he saw mother and son both beaming. That coil in his chest eased. Maybe this hadn't been such a bad idea after all, giving a kid as sweet-natured as Toby a treat while his mom let go of the fear that had to be dogging her nonstop. A break, that was all this was.

Chapter Seven

Erin hated watching Sam drive away later that afternoon. Naturally, she gave a happy wave in case he glanced in his rearview mirror. He'd done so much for them already. How could she beg him not to leave them?

She had to remind herself that there was good reason she hadn't remarried or even wasted time dreaming about meeting the perfect man. Probably because he didn't exist? And after years of building a solid life for herself and her child, she'd hate someone thinking he could make decisions for her.

Okay, just acknowledge it: she was scared. Detective Sam McKeige would come quickly if she called, and that was what she really needed from him. He seemed to genuinely *care*. Giving the time he had to Toby was amazing. She didn't think she'd ever seen Toby more excited than he was when Sam loosened the reins and pushed his gorgeous palomino mare into a lope. Afterward, Toby had grinned, exclaiming, "We galloped! Did you see us, Mommy? Did you?"

Standing in her driveway, feeling bereft for no excusable reason, she smiled at the memory.

And instead of Toby going straight down for his nap when they got home, he thrust out his lower lip and insisted on waiting until Sam reappeared half an hour later and backed into their driveway with a brand new door. It was in the bed of a pickup that must be what Sam drove when he wasn't on the job.

Toby was almost as interested in the construction project as he'd been in the horses. Especially since Sam was nice enough to let him "help."

Sam would be an amazing father. Except...there was something in his eyes that he tried to hide. Pain that she understood in a way she wished she didn't. If Erin lost Toby... She shuddered.

She did her best to put Sam out of her mind and went to work, first using soap and water to clean gray fingerprint powder off the door between the house and garage and numerous plastic tubs that had been dumped. The broken door had been dusted for fingerprints, too, but Sam had tossed it in the bed of his pickup and said he'd "take care of it." She didn't know if that meant throw it away or save it as evidence, but she decided not to worry about it.

Next she went through boxes she'd bought at a recent storage facility auction. She could at least separate those out from garage and yard sale stuff, which she'd boxed herself. Or older purchases that didn't look very exciting and had therefore gotten buried at the back of the garage. She studied, photographed and researched a few pieces of furniture, too, then had to decide which should go to the mall and which be sold online.

Toby was his usual patient self once he woke up and had a snack. She indulged him with a game of hide-and-seek, first in the house with her being the one who hid, then a second round in the garage where there were entirely too many nooks and crannies he could squirm into but she couldn't. They did this often enough she'd gotten to know many of his favorite hidey-holes, but as she shifted furniture and boxes around, adding and taking away, she created new places for him to hide.

Unfortunately, the rocking horse caught his attention again. Given his excitement about horses and galloping, she reluctantly allowed him to ride it.

"We can put it in my room, can't we, Mommy?" he begged, finally getting off.

Dollar signs danced in her eyes, but she recognized true love when she saw it. He'd understand if she said no and explained how much they needed money for rent and groceries and gas for the car—she never mentioned the still tiny savings account she'd started with college for him in mind—but there was something magical about this horse.

It was taller than modern ones she'd seen, carved entirely out of wood with joints so skillfully made, they were hardly visible. The intricate paint job, the genuine leather saddle with stirrups just right for Toby, the leather ears that were getting just a little floppy, combined into something she'd never be able to give him again. It was meant to be an heirloom, she thought. It could be one for her and Toby. She imagined bringing it out of storage for his children and closed her eyes.

"Yes. Okay. It's beautiful, isn't it?"

"Uh-*huh*!" He danced around her and wrapped both arms around her thigh in a hard hug.

She opened her mouth to beg him to be careful with the rocking horse, then managed to make herself shut it again. You couldn't give something wonderful to a three-year-old and then ruin it for them by making them promise never to crash into it with another toy or scratch it or rock so hard those perfect joints started to separate.

She had to let it go. Once she carried it into his room, it would be his. It would still be beautiful when he outgrew it, she convinced herself. *Think how many children have probably already enjoyed it.*

Toby was so happy with the new addition to his room, he let her work in peace for a good hour before he reappeared.

"Can we show it to Sam?" he asked, breaking her train of thought. "He'd like it. Wouldn't he, Mom?"

"We may not see him again," she cautioned. "He was here for special reasons. But yes, I'm sure he'd like it." Seeing his mouth open again, she knew distraction was needed. "Maybe you should name your horse."

"Yeah!"

Of course, he immediately began trying out names, which made it impossible to concentrate on work, so she gave up and put on dinner.

TWO DAYS LATER, Erin opened a cheap plastic tub she'd hauled in from the garage. It was a little grungy, not uncommon when it might have sat in a storage unit for years, and one corner was crumpling as if someone had either piled too much weight on top of it or sat on it before discovering it wasn't sturdy enough.

She'd dropped Toby off at Mrs. Hall's for the morning, giving her much-needed uninterrupted hours to work her way through as much stuff as possible. Something that the black-masked man wanted enough to be willing to set a fire and leave an injured man to die in it was here in her house—well, probably in her house.

She never quite forgot the urgency. It nudged at her, even

when she was playing a silly game with Toby or restocking her booth at the mall or standing in line at the post office to mail items people had purchased on eBay.

Sam had called yesterday to check in. His tone had been courteous but not warm. He was sending a message, she assumed, feeling a little hurt but understanding. He hadn't had any intention of getting involved with her and Toby. It was just the middle-of-the-night scare and an apparent weakness for small boys.

She pried the top off the box and set it aside. At first sight, the contents weren't promising. Although that might not be fair, since everything was jumbled together. It might have been packed carefully, once upon a time, but upended a few times since. She first lifted out a scarf and saw that it was cheap polyester. Thrift store, she decided without hesitation. A second equally cheap one was stained. Throw away.

It was really a rather strange conglomeration. No, that wasn't right—everything appeared to have belonged to a woman, but if so, her tastes had varied wildly. Soft and pastel here, loud and vulgar there. Costume jewelry, and some jewelry well worth the time to clean up and sell. A sandwich bag held a pair of earrings that almost had to be emeralds; the setting was certainly fourteen or even eighteen karat gold. Oddly, there was clothing amid the jumble: a pair of stained leggings—why would anyone have put *them* in storage?—a couple of blouses and near the bottom a bra.

She didn't really want to touch that but picked it up gingerly between her index finger and thumb. It was blue satin, slightly discolored as if from sweat. She dropped it in the black trash bag she always had beside her workspace.

Peering at the items that had worked their way to the

bottom of the tub, she was tempted to just dump them out. But some of it was jewelry, and she'd have to look closely at that. A few single earrings didn't match any she'd already looked at, and a delicate chain that might be gold had tiny links clogged with…something. Her nose crinkled. Suntan lotion, maybe?

She picked up a yellowing box that probably once held a new watch or the like and removed the lid. Even though she had no idea what she was looking at, she recoiled. It was…organic. She thought. Like flesh but mummified. She reluctantly stuck her nose close to take a whiff but was unable to smell anything except the musty odor held by everything in the tub.

Her skin actually crawled as she studied this downright creepy item someone had thought worthy of saving. It lay on a bed of the cushy white stuff that came in jewelry boxes, only this was stained, too, in an unpleasant rusty color. If she didn't know better, she'd think this was…a tongue.

Erin might have squealed as she shoved her chair back. Later, she was glad no one was there to hear her. She was being ridiculously squeamish, but—

She made herself look again, and her stomach turned.

Sam might think she was making an excuse to get him back here, but she didn't know what else to do but to call him. Even he'd agreed that sooner or later she would likely come across something that would be out of the ordinary… and this certainly was.

Sam had been talking to the owner of a rental equipment business in town when his phone rang. A chain-link fence had been cut, and several expensive ride-on mowers as well as a small tractor had been stolen last night. The owner of the business was furious. Sure, he had insurance, but both mowers had been reserved for this weekend, and he might lose good customers when he didn't have the equipment ready when they needed it.

Sam glanced down at his phone, intending to ignore the call, but when he saw Erin's name, he changed his mind.

"Excuse me. I need to take this call," he said. The guy nodded, and Sam walked away. "Erin?"

"I...found something strange. Maybe strange. I can't be sure, but—"

"Whoa. What can be maybe strange, but you don't know?"

"I..." A huff of breath, and then she said more steadily, "I think it might be a tongue. It's all dried up, like mummified or something, and it could be from an animal of some kind. I probably freaked out for no reason, but—"

Feeling grim, he said, "I really doubt you did." She'd taken the horrifying events of the last week better than he'd have expected. Probably because she couldn't afford to break down, not when her son needed her. "Was this... tongue in with other things?"

"Yes, and it was an odd mix. I was already wondering."

"Okay," he said. "Don't touch anything you haven't already. I'm speaking with a business owner who had some equipment stolen last night, but it shouldn't take me long to finish up here. I assume you're home?"

"Yes. I was going to go get Toby, but... I'll call the day-care operator. She'll be fine with me leaving him longer."

Sam finished his report and decided the dollar amount of what had been stolen here justified bringing out a technician to look for fingerprints. There were only a couple of surfaces on padlocks that had been cut and left that could possibly hold a print, but it was worth a try. They'd find fingerprints, but only ones belonging to customers and employees, just as the tech had determined, after getting elimination prints from Erin, that only her prints were on the doors on each side of her garage.

Then he drove barely within the speed limit to Erin's overstuffed ranch-style home. He wanted to use lights and siren to get there faster but knew his sense of urgency wasn't matched by the facts.

Still, he was glad when she opened the door immediately after he rang. Her stress showed, but he also resisted yanking her into his arms the way he had last time. He needed to think about the uncomfortable intensity of emotion he felt for Erin before he acted on it.

"Thank you for coming right away," she said, backing up to let him in. "It's in the dining room."

"I'll want to look at everything that was packed with it." She nodded.

A small box, maybe four inches each way, sat in front of a chair where she'd probably been working.

Erin gestured at it. "I…didn't want to keep looking at it."

"Was it in this box?"

"Yes."

He pulled some latex gloves from his pocket and donned them before carefully taking the top from the box. Then he stared. She might be right. Yes, it could conceivably be from an animal, but…it looked just the right size for a human tongue that had shriveled as its moisture content dissipated.

Riveted on the sight, she said, "I don't know why it didn't rot."

"He may have kept it in a drier place initially. And it

goes to show that the storage unit was solid. No leaks, kept above any rainwater on the asphalt."

He started by taking a couple of photos before carefully restoring the lid to the small box and setting it inside a paper evidence bag. Then he let her show him everything else she'd found in the dirty plastic tub, taking photos as they went.

He agreed with her that the items didn't seem to have belonged to the same woman. The stain on the leggings was highly suggestive. He folded them into a bag, too. He couldn't be sure about the gold chain, but he had a bad feeling that it was skin cells and maybe blood embedded in the tiny links. That one, too, got its own bag. A lot of the rest, he decided to pack back into the original tub, which might still hold fingerprints.

"I'll have to take this with me," he said. "I'll give you a receipt. You'll have to itemize the things you think may be valuable."

She gazed into the tub, an expression of repulsion on her face, but nodded at last. "There are only a few things. Those earrings, for one."

He nodded. They'd caught his eye, too.

He carried the tub out and locked it in the cargo section of his department SUV, then came back with the form he needed her to fill out. She jotted down only a couple of items and handed the pen back to him.

"Honestly, if I never see any of this again, it's fine. I just…have a really bad feeling about it all."

"I understand," he said. "I'll take the tongue to the medical examiner first and have it identified, then send the rest to the crime lab. I hope they don't take too long."

She was wringing her fine-boned fingers together. Anxiety and horror hadn't made her any less beautiful, even knowing she wasn't the kind of woman who usually turned heads. His had turned the minute he set eyes on her.

Yeah, he had to deal with this. He doubted she'd be interested in a short-lived relationship that required her to sneak away when she could take some time or invite him into her bedroom across the hall from her little boy's. He wouldn't be so drawn to her if she was. Her fierce love for Toby was part of what made her so attractive. Nothing subtle about that.

"Okay," he said. "Where was this box?"

"The living room. I'll show you." She led the way.

He didn't see anything he'd call a gap, and none of the nearby tubs were the same color or as dirty. Nonetheless, still wearing the gloves, he lifted lids on every nearby tub.

Nothing seemed obviously related to either of them.

"I'm sorry," she said. "They all look so much alike, you know."

Having seen the treasure trove in her garage and house, he did know.

"Why would a single box from a unit have been separated from the rest of the contents?"

She crinkled her nose. "When either I or the two guys I hire unload stuff, I don't have any *reason* to keep things from a particular source separate. Furniture sets tend to get put together, but cardboard boxes or plastic tubs?" She shook her head. "It's wherever there's room. And I was thinking today—"

When she broke off, he said, "You were thinking?"

"Well, Toby and I were playing hide-and-seek. He almost always wins when we play in the garage, because there are plenty of tunnels between piles and probably even some mazes out there. But what occurred to me today is that, while I get to know some of his favorite spots, they change regularly. I remove boxes or bigger items, replace them, wedge a tub in someplace without a thought."

"In other words," Sam said, "your maze shifts from day to day."

"Exactly. It never occurred to me it would matter where I put any particular thing. Well, except when I knew it would be valuable, like the furniture I showed you."

"And the rocking horse."

Now, she really looked chagrined. "I succumbed to Toby's begging and let him have it. It's in his room—and has a name."

He raised his eyebrows.

"It's a girl, he says. She's Rosie."

"He doesn't think his buddies will make fun of that?"

"I did hint at that, but... Well, he only has one good friend from his daycare, and Austin has never been here."

"Ah." Did she *ever* invite anyone to her house?

"It's only been this last year that my, um, backlog has spilled into the house. And... I know it's sort of strange and probably makes me look like a hoarder, so no, I don't like people to see." She was talking faster and faster. "But while I'm not swearing off auctions, I'm resolved to be way pickier so I can catch up enough to make our house livable again."

He laid a hand on her arm. "Erin."

She looked as if she'd braced herself.

"Your house is clean, and you and Toby *don't* need much space. I'm not judging you. I understand why you've accumulated so much. In fact, I admire you for making a solid living from your skill at judging what's valuable or at least will appeal to shoppers. Don't apologize for that."

Her relaxation was subtle, but her smile was pure sunshine. "Thank you." Then she made a face. "I'm always thanking you!"

Amused, he said, "Then knock it off. And remind yourself that I'm doing my job. Mostly," he added but could tell she heard only that he was being paid to help her out.

She squared her shoulders, nodded and smiled again, but only pleasantly. "Will you keep me informed?"

"You know I will. It occurs to me, though, that we may need to get prints from the guys who haul stuff for you."

She shook her head. "They always wear leather work gloves. I've seen them take them off to open a can of pop or when they're driving, but never when they're loading or unloading. Also, I've never seen either of them peel the top off a tub. So if you find fingerprints inside the one you just took, they're either mine or the previous owner's."

"Okay," he said with nod. "You wouldn't have purchased from a unit that consisted of only a few plastic tubs, would you? I'm assuming there are a whole lot of boxes, furniture, whatever, from the same unit."

"That's true," she agreed. "I mean, unless that tub came from a garage sale where I offered money for the contents of a few boxes they maybe hadn't even set out yet? That happens."

"Is it likely?"

She frowned. "Probably not. Nothing looked that appealing when I opened the tub. I don't remember it, either, which I think I would if I'd bought the stuff individually. Truthfully, I haven't done that kind of thing in a while. I'm doing better with the auctions. Older garage sale stuff

I haven't gotten to would likely be in the back in the garage. And anyway..."

Sam grimaced. "We know the man who attacked Jeremy Conyers was after his possessions that had been sold from that particular facility."

"Right."

"Well, not meaning to nag, but I hope you'll try to find the rest of the stuff from the same storage space."

"Of course I will. Here, let me walk you out."

He missed feeling the warmth but told himself it was just as well she'd taken what he said as a warning. Even so, he was as reluctant to leave her as he'd been every other time.

Traffic was heavy enough once he reached the highway to require his concentration, however. He radioed in his intentions so Dispatch knew he wouldn't be immediately available and headed for Everett, where the medical examiner's office was located.

He arrived just as a jet took off from Paine Field, close enough to make him want to duck, and carried the tub in. Given that the day was winding down, he was grateful that an investigator was willing to take a look immediately... and even more grateful when the young woman looked up at him with a faint hint of shock and said, "The medical examiner needs to look at this."

She disappeared for about ten minutes, then returned with the older man who was the current county medical examiner. He nodded, bent close to study the tongue and said, "I'd like to look at this under a microscope."

There was one in the room, not surprisingly, along with equipment Sam didn't recognize. He'd attended autopsies here, but his errand today was unusual.

"It's certainly a tongue," the pathologist agreed, "and I'm almost certain it's human. Given the context… Well."

Sam nodded, then showed them the necklace, too.

Those were definitely human cells trapped in the links, the medical examiner confirmed after studying it under the microscope.

In the end, Sam left both items with them in hopes DNA would give him some answers and took everything else with him, including the items with stains. Fingerprints on anything in the tub—or *on* the tub—would be more helpful right now. DNA results were too slow, even if the medical examiner had agreed that the attacks and break-ins suggested answers were needed *now*…before someone died.

Chapter Eight

Erin was helping Toby buckle into his booster seat when her phone rang. Oh, goody. She didn't much want to deal with *anyone* right now…except Sam McKeige, whose name showed up on the screen.

She closed the car door so Toby wouldn't be able to hear what she said. "Sam?"

"Yeah. I stopped at the medical examiner's office. They're confident the tongue is human and plan to extract DNA and send it off."

Hearing an undertone, she said, "That's what you wanted, isn't it?"

"Except that results will take months. And then if there's no match in any database…"

"Oh." He wasn't telling her anything she didn't already know from the mysteries she read. "Then it's not much help, is it?"

"We may get lucky." He didn't sound convinced. "I've just parked to drop off the other stuff at our evidence unit. Fingerprints could give us a direction a lot sooner." He paused. "Did you have a chance to hunt anymore?"

"No, I had to do a couple of quick errands, then pick up Toby at Mrs. Hall's. I'm standing outside her house right now." Toby had seemed awfully glad to see her. She sighed. "I shouldn't have left him so long."

"At least he's not stuck in daycare full-time."

"No, that's true, but the only boy his age—"

"Austin?"

"What a memory! Austin's mom moved him to a bigger, commercial daycare. I may have to do the same but—" What was she doing? The detective was not her best friend eager to listen to all her confidences. "I'm sorry. Um, thank you for—"

He cleared his throat, and she chuckled.

"For calling."

"Yeah." He was quiet for a minute. "Do you have dinner planned?"

"Not really," she admitted. Was he—?

"What if I pick up a pizza and bring it by? Does Toby like pizza?"

"As long as it's cheese only." She felt a foolish smile spread. "We'd love that."

He wanted to know her preferences, and they came to an agreement. She was still grinning when the call ended. Earlier, she could have sworn he was warning her off, but she had to have misread him. Her giddiness was absurd considering her own determination to be uninterested in Sam anyway.

And then there was the rest of her day so far…and the reason she'd had to call him.

Her smile dwindled. At least Toby would be thrilled.

SAM CALLED IN the order during his drive back across the trestle over the Snohomish River and the wetlands surrounding it. Technically, he'd finished his working day, but for a detective, that meant nothing. He considered a forty-hour workweek to be a vacation.

He'd left a message yesterday for Jeremy Conyers, who apparently wasn't eager to call back. Until now, it seemed...

Sam tapped his phone. "Mr. Conyers?"

"This a bad time?"

"No, I'm driving but have hands-free."

"I went back to work today, but you know what the office looked like." Conyers gusted out a breath. "I'm paying a nephew and a friend of his to help clean up and haul crap out to the dumpster. So far, I've recovered a few records but not many, and none that would interest you."

"Because they're for on-going rentals?"

"Right. I've got the computer in at a shop, but they don't know yet how much they can save. And even if they succeed, I only began using it recently. My uncle's business practices were at least fifty years out of date. I hadn't even started entering the paper records, so I'm not sure how much help I'll be."

"What about records for the units where you auctioned off the contents? Wouldn't that be in the computer? If they were recent?"

"No." Conyers sounded as glum as Sam was starting to feel. "Those units were all ones where nobody had been paying for a while. I don't know if Uncle Charles hadn't noticed—he was kind of losing it—but I could tell we hadn't received payment for six months or more. I still sent off a late bill to each address, including a warning that the contents would be auctioned off. When there was no response or the bill was returned to me, I went ahead. All I did was make a note in each file of how much I received and the check number. Far as I can tell, that all burned."

"You sounded as if you thought there might be old records at your uncle's house," Sam reminded him.

"It's conceivable. What I had for those units was skimpy.
If he kept older files, I might find more." After another
sigh, Conyers said, "Give me a couple of days, and I'll do
some digging at Uncle Charles's house. Man, I haven't even
started there. It doesn't look as if he and Aunt Marie ever
threw a thing away."

"That's tough." Sam could empathize, but the problem
wasn't one he would ever face. His mother was dead, and
he and his father were estranged. Sam wasn't even sure
he'd hear if or when his dad died. "I hate to keep pushing,
but like I said, Ms. Reed had a frightening break-in during
the night when the intruder had to know she and her boy
were home. She scared him off, but I'm sure he'll be back."

"I'll do my best," Conyers said, about the same time Sam
reached the riverfront town of Snohomish.

Once he'd picked up the pizza from his favorite parlor,
he headed east along the valley, brooding about his sudden turnaround. He'd resolved to keep some distance, and
usually his self-discipline was better than this. The trouble
was, he wanted to be close to Erin, not the opposite. If it
weren't for her boy—

A car passed him on the two-lane freeway driving way
too fast and barely able to make it around his vehicle and
back in his lane before an oncoming semi would have flat-
tened it. Sam wanted to turn on the lights and at least ticket
the fool, but he was tired and didn't want the pizza to get
cold. How did anybody drive this stretch of the highway
without seeing all the warnings? Drivers were requested
to turn their headlights on even in the daytime. With the
highway raised because of frequent flooding, there was

nowhere to pull off. More head-on collisions occurred on this stretch of road than anywhere else in the county, but people didn't seem to learn.

Sam's thoughts returned to his unaccountable weakness where Erin was concerned...or maybe it was about her three-year-old son. Or both.

Part of it, he knew, came from the dread that had taken up residence under his breastbone. A hard knot of worry. Jeremy Conyers would be dead...if Erin hadn't intervened. Kevin Hargrove would be dead if he'd happened to arrive home when a stranger was in his garage smashing things to vent frustration. If that same stranger had been able to break in to Erin's home from the garage, *she* might be dead.

Even before her discovery today, Sam had been working this investigation harder than he might normally when it wasn't a murder.

Yet.

Sam knew Erin was at the heart of this ongoing string of crimes. Once this scum eliminated other eBay sellers, he'd circle back to Erin. He'd seen her garage now and possibly guessed that she had more in her house. If she had what he considered his, he probably wouldn't be able to find it without her guidance, something he wouldn't get without threats or the point of a knife or barrel of a gun.

What would happen when he got to her and found out *she* couldn't find what he was looking for? *That* was what scared Sam. Especially since she had a huge vulnerability: that cute little boy.

Sam wondered whether there was an ex-husband who'd be able to take Toby for a few weeks.

After pulling into Erin's driveway and parking beside her pickup truck, setting the brake and killing the engine, he rubbed at the ache in his chest with the heel of his hand. He'd ask her about the boy's dad, but he'd be surprised if the guy was in the picture at all. When she talked about setting out on her new career, Sam had heard the trace of desperation. Monthly payments from the ex would provide a cushion he felt sure she didn't have.

He grabbed the pizza box and got out.

ERIN RETURNED FROM tucking Toby in for the night to find Sam had put the leftover pizza in the fridge and was loading their few dishes after rinsing them.

"Thank you. Can I offer you a cup of coffee?"

"No, I should get home," he said, closing the dishwasher. "I want to talk to you about a couple of things, though."

She stayed on her feet, wary of where the conversation was about to go. "Okay."

"First, I plan to come back in the morning if that works for you and help go through boxes. I may bring in another officer, too."

She opened her mouth, then closed it. "It's important whoever is here is careful."

"That goes without saying."

Did it?

"The tongue was all the way at the bottom of that tub. Would the other stuff have caught your eye? I mean, I often go through one of those tubs wondering why anyone bothered saving a single thing in it. Another one with…with…"

"What might be a serial killer's trophies?"

He hadn't put it that bluntly before, but she'd considered the same possibility, too.

"It won't be that easy to pick out, that's all," she said.

"I get that, Erin." He had a gentle tone that she'd never

be able to resist. "Two of us working at a time has to be faster than you going at it alone."

"Yes. Okay."

He shifted, rolling his shoulders in a betrayal of some discomfort. "Something else I wanted to ask. Is Toby's father around? Or any grandparents? I'm thinking someplace he could go stay for a couple of weeks."

Erin shook her head. "Shawn dodges paying child support. He hasn't seen Toby since he was a baby."

Sam no doubt had to hear stories like that all the time, but his mouth tightened anyway.

"My parents were killed in a car accident," she continued. "Missing them was probably one reason I got married too quickly. And Shawn's dad...no."

"All right. Just a thought." There it was again, a note she'd almost call tenderness, especially coupled with the softening of his expression. The expression returned to cop-neutral as if he'd flipped a switch. "Expect me between eight and nine, if that's not too early."

"Nope. Toby is a 6:00 a.m. alarm clock."

He chuckled. "That doesn't surprise me."

Moments later, he was gone, and she was left to study the piles of plastic tubs almost as tall as her that filled the living room. She'd have to follow his example—not waste time evaluating individual items, probably even sorting them. For now, their only goal would be finding anything else that qualified as creepy.

Should she plan to take Toby to Mrs. Hall's tomorrow, maybe for the whole day? He wouldn't like it, but it would free her and Sam—no, *call him the detective*, since he'd be on the job—to concentrate. On the other hand, Toby did entertain himself well, and she could take her usual breaks to play a game.

That was what they'd do, unless Toby bugged Sam too much or got whiny. Those were the moments when she most appreciated Mrs. Hall's open drop-in policy.

She felt a pang as she wondered if she'd ever see Sam again once he succeeded in arresting the horrible man who'd left Jeremy to die in the fire and was now terrorizing her.

She made a face at what amounted to a moment of sheer fantasy. There was only one priority right now: finding out who had broken into her house, thereby ensuring Toby's and her safety.

What were the chances she'd get any sleep tonight, after last night's terrifying interlude?

SAM HADN'T TOLD Erin that he intended to park somewhere on her block to keep an eye on her house that night. He would let himself doze but no more. The sound of a vehicle engine anywhere in the vicinity should awaken him, and how would anybody enter her house silently?

With her front door solid and the door into the garage now steel with a dead bolt, the one vulnerability was the kitchen door leading to the backyard. While it wasn't steel, it had a dead bolt, too. Kicking it in wouldn't happen quietly. Breaking a window seemed logical, and he believed he'd hear that as long as he left his own window cracked.

He'd have rather guarded her and Toby from the inside, but asking to move in seemed over the top. That much closeness held a different kind of risk, too. Now that he knew the skimpiness of the knit boxers and thin tank top that she slept in, he imagined coming face-to-face with her in the middle of the night when she'd just come out of the bathroom. He could keep his hands off her despite temptation…but why set himself up like that?

Best not to put himself in that position.

He went home, showered and ate, then drove back to her block. As her neighbor had pointed out, there weren't many cars parked at the curb versus in driveways. That might make him conspicuous, but he doubted the creep had surveyed the area enough to know which vehicles belonged and which didn't.

He laid his seat back in hopes a casual glance would make his truck look empty, then closed his eyes and tried for the shallow sleep that usually came easily. Not tonight.

He had only two brief alarms during the night. A car crept by so slowly, he came to an instant state of alertness. Not a big black SUV, he noted, watching as it continued onto the next block. The driver was having trouble maintaining a straight line. Drunk seemed likely. Sam's debate about whether he had to pull the car over ended when a garage door opened in the middle of the next block, the car made it in—lucky it was an otherwise empty two-car garage—and the door closed behind it.

The second time, he lifted heavy eyelids to see a flicker of movement in the front yard of a house a couple doors down from Erin's. A dog, he finally realized, a big one. It was sniffing and peeing its way along, presumably an escapee from its own yard.

The pale light of dawn killed any last hopes of more sleep for Sam, who groaned, ran a hand over his face and started the engine. He'd get a breakfast sandwich at a fast-food joint, then come back. Since he'd shaved last evening, he hoped it wouldn't be obvious to Erin that he had done anything but sleep in his own bed.

When Erin let him in half an hour later, she looked even more tired than he felt: puffy eyes with bruised circles under them, her movements slow enough he suspected she was on autopilot. Guilt struck; if he'd slept in her house again, *she* would have slept, too. They'd both be more efficient today.

He'd have to think about that.

"Coffee?" she asked.

He'd had a cup of crap brew from the fast-food restaurant. "Thanks," he said.

She turned without another word and headed for the kitchen. He heard a tuneless form of singing coming from that direction in a high voice.

"Jingle bells, jingle bells, jingle all away."

Amusement improved Sam's mood. "He's ready for Christmas?" It was still months away.

She made a sound in her throat. "A little early. And unfortunately, that's the only part of the song he remembers."

Somewhat imperfectly.

"Jingle bells, jingle bells, jingle... Mommy!" Kneeling on a chair, his elbows planted on the table, Toby grinned. "Sam!"

"Yep. You're bright-eyed and bushy-tailed this morning."

"I don't have a tail! Why'd you say I had a tail?"

Sam let out a sigh he tried to keep soundless, but Erin gave him a sidelong look of sympathy. He didn't know the origin of the saying himself but had heard it had something to do with... "Squirrels. Always bright-eyed and how they flick their tails like they're ready to go at any minute."

"They are fast," Toby conceded.

Erin had shuffled over to the coffeepot and was pouring what he presumed was a second or even third cup for her and one for him.

"Toby staying home today?" Sam asked.

"We'll see how it goes," she said.

"What do you mean, Mom? You *said*—"

Her turn to sigh. Sam grinned.

Two hours later, he still had his audience. Erin had dragged a couple of tubs to the table, one for her to start with, the second for him. Toby had decided Sam was more interesting than his mother and had queried Sam about nearly everything he removed from the tub. Erin eventually squelched that, but Toby still watched with interest. As Sam packed everything back in the third tub he'd dug through, Toby said, "Mommy, can I go ride my horse?"

"Sure you can." She held out an arm. "Hug me first." Once Toby had trotted away down the hall, she said, "Thanks for being so patient. I know he's a lot."

Sam shook his head. "He's a good kid. I haven't heard him whine yet."

"Oh, he's capable, but he doesn't do it a lot. Toby was born cheerful."

"Isn't the first thing a baby does is cry?" As if he didn't know. Hearing Michael's first cry, he would have sworn his heart had doubled in size. Dr. Seuss had gotten that one right.

"Well, yeah, but you know what I mean. When I took him out, he'd grin at every person he saw. He never had the 'stranger danger' phase that most babies and toddlers have."

"I remember that—" He all but bit his tongue, he cut himself off so fast.

She'd quit working and watched him, her eyes compassionate. But she didn't say a word. Obviously, she wasn't going to push.

Maybe that was why he heard himself say, "I had a son. I told you that, didn't I?" He cleared roughness from his voice. "He...was killed when he was four."

"Oh, Sam," she said softly, reaching across the table to touch the back of his hand. "I'm so sorry."

He turned it over and gripped her hand. "It was tough. He...was with his mother. We were separated. She'd been drinking heavily. I never thought she'd drive drunk with him in the car but—" Man, he couldn't find the next words. The real next words were, *I'd have done anything. I* would *do anything.* Meaningless, when you couldn't go back.

"I can't let myself imagine." Her eyes darkened. Then tiny creases formed on her forehead, and she said, "That's why you're worrying so much about Toby and me, isn't it? Because...because of your son."

Of course it was. Partly. "He reminded me of Michael at first, but not so much as I've gotten to know him. You're right. Toby is pure sunshine."

"I will never understand."

He took the same jump she had, to the ex, a guy who'd walked away from his own child. "I can't either," he agreed. What kind of man did that?

"I tell myself it's his loss." Erin lifted one shoulder. "Except Toby's lost something, too."

"I'm not seeing it. He's happy because he has everything he needs here with you, Erin. He might have questions later, but he's not mourning a father who is not in his life, or you'd know it."

"Look how he latches onto you. That tells me something."

"It may just be that I'm new." For her sake, he hoped that was the case.

Darkness shadowed her eyes for a moment. "I hope it was fast. What happened to your little boy."

"So I was told. Mostly I try not to dwell, but—"

"Toby reminded you. I'm sorry about that, too."

The words that came out of his mouth startled him. "I'm not."

Chapter Nine

He blinked, then frowned. Finally, voice hoarse again, he added, "I've tried not to be around kids. I thought I'd just be punishing myself. But Toby… He's his own person." He shrugged. "At first I thought about Michael. Now, I just see Toby."

"I'm glad," she said.

He shook himself. Time to rebuild his wall. "I'm ready for a new tub. Does it matter which one I grab?"

"Oh…we can probably skip some. I'm done with this one, too."

He waited until she'd put the top back on hers, then took it before she could stand, piled it atop his and lifted both.

"I could have—"

He lifted his brows.

"You know I haul stuff all day, every day."

"Yeah, but I'm here right now."

She rolled her eyes and led the way to the living room, where a small gap showed where they'd pulled out these boxes.

He added the two he carried to a new pile they'd started, then said, "Any two?"

"No, we can skip this one. I glanced in it earlier—it's Christmas ornaments."

The tub itself was bright red with a green top. Out of curiosity, he peeled off the lid to see that cardboard dividers and layers of cardboard protected a large tree's worth of delicate ornaments. "Huh," he said. "I've seen these for sale in the hardware store before Christmas."

She gave him a strange look. "Doesn't everyone pack their ornaments in one of these?"

"I don't usually bother with a tree," he said shortly. He and Ashley had gone to her parents' for the holidays every year, killing a good part of his annual vacation, but it was important to her, and having grandparents mattered to Michael, so Sam had never complained. "Do you have one of these boxes?" he asked, but then wished he hadn't. The topic was irrelevant to their task and to his job. He still hadn't come to terms with the idea of getting too personal with Erin.

"Sure. Last year, I let Toby pick out a new ornament. I thought I'd make it an annual tradition." She shrugged. "The ornaments in there—" she nodded to the bright plastic tub "—look especially high quality. I might keep a few. Otherwise, I'll make a display of Christmas decorations at the antique mall when we get closer to the holidays."

"That makes sense." He looked around. "Do you have any suggestions, or do we need to go through them all?"

"I see others that I packed myself from garage sale purchases, or that I glanced at already, but for now—" She grimaced.

"Got it." He chose two at random, discovering the second was seriously heavy.

"What?" she asked.

"Feels like it's full of bricks."

"Hmm." Erin removed the top, and they both stared

in at a couple of concrete figurines. "Garden sculptures. Those'll go fast." She sounded delighted. "Let's put this one by the front door."

He shook his head and hefted it himself. "Why don't you let me load it in your truck?"

"Thank you. I may as well take advantage of your strong back."

She lowered the tailgate, watched him heave the box in, then closed it again.

Inside, they took a couple of more tubs and carried them into the kitchen.

"This one's dirty," he commented.

"Like the one with the tongue." She eyed it when he set it beside his chair. "You're right, but it's not the same color."

"Does anybody buy all matching ones when they decide to store a bunch of their possessions?"

She made a face. "Mostly not. I suspect a lot of people start with a unit when they're moving, then keep adding to it instead of closing it. Or else they buy more plastic tubs when they've filled the first ones, or see a sale."

A grunt expressed his opinion of paying monthly for years to store stuff you didn't need or even want in your home.

She'd had the same thought, of course, given that emptying those units in the end gave her a livelihood. But what a waste for the original owners.

SAM HAD JUST finished his second molasses cookie following the sandwich Erin had fed him for lunch when his phone rang. He'd been surprised to make it undisturbed through the morning.

He answered and walked into the living room for the

brief conversation. Deputy Warren had been called to a home that had been burglarized, and he thought Sam might be interested.

Sam didn't have to ask why. It wasn't hard to guess. Sam thanked him and said he'd be right there.

He went back to the kitchen, where Erin was rinsing the plates and Toby crumbled the remains of a cookie he hadn't been able to finish. Both gazes went right to Sam.

"I knew I'd get pulled away sooner or later. I need to talk to my lieutenant about assigning someone else to help you, too. For now, I'll try to get back this afternoon but can't promise."

"I'll just keep on," she said, sounding undaunted—or maybe just determined to remind him that she usually worked alone.

"Okay." He ruffled Toby's hair, then glanced at Erin. "Lock behind me?"

"Oh, sure."

Almost to the front door, she said, "Is this thing you're leaving for related?"

"Probably not, but I have everyone on alert."

She gave him a sturdy nod.

Sam yearned to stay. It was all he could do not to reach for her. To touch her, one way or another. Her eyes widened as he betrayed more than he'd intended, but he made himself nod, open the door and go without looking back.

The address he'd been given wasn't half a mile away. Sam parked at the curb and walked up the driveway.

Ed Warren stuck his head out of the side door into the garage and waved to get his attention. "Thought I heard you."

The moment Sam stepped into the garage, a place of shadows since it was lit by a single bulb dangling from a rafter, he saw why Warren had called him. "Damn," he said softly.

This space wasn't jammed on a scale with Erin's garage, but it was close. His first thought was that the homeowner was also an eBay seller or the like—except as he scanned the contents, it became apparent that furniture took up much of the space in here, along with a washer and dryer not hooked up and of course the ubiquitous plastic tubs along with plenty of packed cardboard boxes.

The tubs and boxes had been dumped, the contents ransacked quite a bit carelessly or otherwise trampled.

"The homeowner have any idea what has been taken?" Sam asked.

"Unfortunately, she doesn't. Her son and daughter-in-law are in Europe—London, where he had a two-year contract position. Mom offered to store their stuff."

Sam winced. "I hope she wasn't home."

"No, thank God. She spent the night in Seattle with her daughter. I don't like to think what would have happened if she'd been home and came out here to see what was going on."

"No." Erin had done the right thing. Sam's guess was that this was a more typical burglary, and the perp might have run rather than attack, but...there was a lot of destruction out here, too. He shook his head. "I don't think this is the same guy that broke into Ms. Reed's garage, but this is a step up from our usual burglaries where someone just grabs some electronics."

"That was my feeling," the deputy agreed.

"I haven't heard of anything else like this," Sam commented. "Have you?"

"I hadn't, but while I was waiting for you, I called Snohomish PD and spoke to a detective there. They had a break-in a couple weeks ago that sounds a lot like this. Didn't come up with a witness or fingerprints, unfortunately."

Which likely meant the sheriff's department wouldn't, either, but they had to try.

"You call for a fingerprint tech?"

"On their way. We're keeping them busy in our little corner of the county," Warren said dryly.

"Yes, we are. Do you need me?"

"No, just wanted you to see it."

Sam took a last, frowning look around. "Keep me informed, would you?"

"Sure thing."

Warren was a good cop. Sam wondered if he'd applied for promotion to the detective division. He might not be interested—but Sam would have to ask him.

Didn't it figure, his phone rang again before he could even get in his vehicle. He wouldn't be making it back to Erin's this afternoon—although he had every intention of spending yet another night parked close by to watch over her house and its occupants.

ERIN HAD THOUGHT everything from the storage unit with the unique and valuable items had been deposited more or less together in her garage. Still, she wasn't surprised when she discovered that wasn't the case.

This tub, she'd found in the living room. Erin had been working her way through everything in this one room to be sure she didn't miss anything. So far, she'd only set a couple of boxes and plastic tubs aside, in both cases because the contents held such obvious appeal she'd want to list them on her eBay site or put them in the antique mall as soon as she had a moment to pursue her actual livelihood.

The moment she pried the top off this tub, she gasped. It was partly filled with books, leather-bound and in beautiful condition. She stroked one of the bindings and handled the books carefully as she lifted them out. Books weren't a specialty of hers; she sold some that she came across, but nothing like this.

Research, she reminded herself.

Carefully rolled in crinkly paper was a scarf with exquisitely detailed birds and flowers embroidered on a cream silk backdrop. Gently laying it out, Erin realized it wasn't intended for a woman to wear, although she certainly could, but rather to lay over the top of an upright piano. Even the fringe was in excellent condition.

She sighed with pleasure and set it aside.

Several more treasures, including a number of other pieces of fabric art: tatted doilies, fringed and lushly decorated scarves that looked designed to cover a small tabletop and so on.

The plastic tub itself looked like some she knew had been piled around the children's rocking horse Toby had so coveted.

Almost to the bottom, she found tied in faded blue ribbon an inch-thick pile of letters. Those she took to the dining room. Even the ink had a different look than was usual now. After untying the ribbon and opening a selection of the letters, she found the handwriting all the same. They also seemed to contain only the first name of the writer and her correspondent. All were addressed to *Dear Kitty*, and signed *With all my love, Winnie*.

She'd have to read the letters with care—the handwrit-

ing was sharply slanted and spidery—to hope to find any
details about where either woman had lived or a last name.
Guiltily, she realized she'd already spent more time on this
one plastic tub than she should have. She'd promised Sam
to ignore anything that she could be certain didn't have
anything to do with the other, odd collection.

Still, she took time to call Jeremy Conyers.

When he answered, he said, "Erin," without a lot of enthusiasm.

"Yes, I just came across some letters in a tub I'm sure
is from that same unit. You know, the one with such beautiful things."

"Which, for reasons I don't get, you want to give *back*
to the family that quit paying the storage rent."

"Well, that's not quite true. But there are some things
that shouldn't have left the family, and…" She stopped.
"Anyway, I came across a possible name, although it's only
a first name. Kitty."

"Kitty."

"From the handwriting, I'm guessing the letters are from
the 1930s or '40s. Maybe even earlier than that. Anyway,
I thought if you happen across that name—"

"Uh-huh. I'll let you know. Although you may have to
wait in line behind that detective. He's not letting up, either."

For which she could only give thanks. "Are you okay?"
she asked tentatively. "You sound tired."

"Not quite myself, but I'm starting to dig into the boxes
my uncle had stored in his garage. I have a feeling I'll be
building a big bonfire in the backyard one of these days.
Why he kept such old records is a mystery to me."

"But that's exactly where you'd find records for this unit!"

He sighed. "Maybe. Just because it's old stuff doesn't mean it's been sitting in that unit for fifty years. Those plastic tubs looked more modern than that, for one thing."

She blinked and focused on the sturdy tub in front of her. It wasn't new, by any means, but when had such things started being manufactured? People had once used wooden trunks, many with arched lids. Cardboard boxes would have come next.

"You're right," she said. "Still."

"I owe you," he said. "I'll keep looking."

"I couldn't have left you," she protested.

"It would have been smarter for you to grab Toby and run. You took a risk," he said gruffly. "I'll never be able to thank you enough."

Before she could open her mouth again, he'd cut the connection.

"I HAVE A rookie for you to borrow," Sam's lieutenant said during their latest phone conversation. "Kid broke his ankle tripping on the stairs downtown."

Sam had heard about that one. Twenty-one or -two, the young deputy would never be permitted to forget his clumsiness.

He wouldn't be able to carry full boxes and tubs for Erin, Sam reflected, but otherwise might be a good choice if he had any kind of eye at all. It wasn't like he could be called out, the way Sam so frequently was, or assigned a regular patrol.

"He's better than nothing," Sam said. "Ah...what's his name?"

"Patrick Knapstad."

"Right. Is he available tomorrow?"

"No, he's in some pain and supposed to stay prone with his foot elevated." The lieutenant sounded disgusted at one of his officers taking it that easy but added, "I'll have him there at eight o'clock Tuesday morning."

The day after tomorrow. Sam hoped the kid actually turned out to be useful.

He wanted to stop by Erin's house and see how much she'd accomplished, get himself invited to dinner—or bring a take-out dinner with him again. He'd been involving himself with her and the boy more than he should, though. He needed to focus on their safety, not making friends...or reaching even beyond that.

Instead he headed home, shoveled some manure from the paddocks and turned the horses out to pasture for to-night and tomorrow. Then he showered and turned on a Mariners baseball game while he ate a sizeable helping of chili that he'd frozen the last time he cooked.

His phone stayed silent. Erin would have called if she'd found anything. He convinced himself nobody would attempt a break-in during daylight. Late afternoon and early evening were the least likely times, given that so many neighbors would be arriving home from work.

When dusk deepened the sky he saw through his front window, he turned off the TV, realizing a minute later he couldn't remember the score. He could turn on the radio in his truck...but this was early enough in the MLB season, there was no point getting excited one way or the other. Funny, when once upon a time, he'd been passionate about the sport.

He'd played on a minor league team for a couple of years, but shoulder damage he'd done playing college ball returned in an ache that required alternating ice and heat to treat after games and even practices. He didn't want his body to break down over a sport. He'd never regretted that decision.

His wife did, though; she'd had visions of her husband pitching in the World Series, making the kind of money most people didn't even dream about. He thought now she'd been drinking too much even before he applied to the police academy and then took a job in a mostly rural county sheriff's department north of Seattle, but things were never the same between them after he gave up on his own boyhood dream of stardom. She drank more, which he hated, and by that time he suspected they stuck together only because of Michael.

Erin was right, he thought, as he made the twenty-minute drive to her place half a dozen blocks from the river. He couldn't deny his attraction to her...but he dreaded thinking what it would do to him to see her bright, optimistic little boy dead.

Once this was over, he should probably back off and stick to his vow never to have children, not when he of all people knew you never got over the devastation of losing one.

Right now, though... Yeah, he'd park outside her house, sitting in darkness hour after hour, just to make sure this piece of scum didn't so much as look in their window.

What he hadn't decided was what he'd do if he got called away.

Chapter Ten

Was it possible for sunny good fortune to shine down on you even as a dark cloud hovered? Erin had no idea. She wished the better-than-ever sales balanced out the fire, the break-in and the ever-present anxiety, but it didn't seem to work that way.

Still, she couldn't help feeling good about her day. The owner of the antique mall had called that morning to let her know the booth beside Erin's had been cleaned out.

"Eleanor says she's going to concentrate on eBay from now on," Marsha said. "She's been putting in a lot of overtime at her day job and hasn't been able to pick up much in the way of new items lately."

The booth had looked picked over for quite a while. Whereas Erin could fill it in a heartbeat.

Well, not quite that, since it required her to load furniture and boxes she already had ready to go. She'd have to haul them to the mall, then go back for another load and another—because it turned out she'd had a stellar weekend of sales in her existing booth and needed to restock it, too.

She ought to stay home doing the task Sam had assigned her, but she needed to keep making a living, too. She'd spend a few hours tonight going through boxes at home, she decided. And she'd taken so much stuff out of her house today, she hoped she could consolidate what was left in the house to clear at least some space, if not a room. Now if she could just find time to list more things online...

Knowing how busy she'd be, she'd taken Toby to Mrs. Hall's for the entire day. She'd promised him they would go out for dinner after she picked him up. She felt guilty watching him trudge in the door with an air of resignation instead of the excitement he'd have felt if Austin had still been there for him to play with.

Some kids had to go to daycare forty hours or more a week, she reminded herself. Mrs. Hall read stories and played games with the children in her daycare; she had a swing set and a sturdy climber with a short slide in her fully fenced backyard. Toby would not be suffering.

The proprietor of another of the more successful booths, Steve Boulton, was leaving just as she arrived. He grabbed a brick to hold open the door for her benefit, then said, "Need a hand?"

"I wouldn't mind one," she admitted.

Steve was in his early sixties but lean and strong. A couple of years ago, he'd told her his history: the company he worked with had gone under, and he'd decided to try the antique business rather than job-hunting. His wife's health wasn't good, and he wanted to be home with her rather than always on the road as he had been.

He carried more than a fair share of the heavier items, moving them as she decided where to put what. He had a good eye, she'd already known, and made a few suggestions.

"Bless you," she said as they parted out back. "I'm off to get another load, but thanks to you I have plenty of energy left over."

He laughed. "And no short helper today, either."

"I figured this would be too full a day for him," she conceded.

After she packed the pickup truck and even the passenger seat beside her as full as she could, Erin made the return trip and unloaded with some help from yet another booth proprietor. Over time, they'd all formed a kind of community that she appreciated. A few months back, she'd caught a browser pocketing jewelry from a booth across from her, and someone else returned the favor for her.

That memory on her mind, she decided to display some especially nice jewelry inside a glass-fronted cabinet that locked. It was a bit of a nuisance for whoever was at the front desk when Erin wasn't here, but she had a price point that separated the small pieces she'd leave unprotected from the items that were worth extra effort. Usually—always on weekends—two people worked the front desk and took turns circulating and helping customers, so it wasn't difficult for a customer to get someone to unlock to show a particular item.

She turned in place, pleased with her effort. Bright pieces of collectible dishware joined quilted placemats and fringed cloth napkins on a table she'd snapped up for next-to-nothing at a yard sale. She'd found a bouquet of silk flowers to display in a tall, distinctive vase she thought completed the effect. Smaller rugs draped over a rack. A beautiful, though worn, Grandmother's Flower Garden quilt lay as if tossed casually over the back of a wing chair, while a copper floor lamp made the corner cozy. Framed prints, porcelain figurines, some antique kitchen tools and more had their spots. She'd even found a place for a lawn mower and for a few yard tools—and one of the two concrete garden sculptures. She didn't expect any of the yard stuff to last through the weekend.

Marsha came by to admire her effort and give her a nice check for the previous week's sales. As a result, Erin was feeling good when she picked up Toby half an hour later.

He waffled on the dinner selection but finally decided on chicken nuggets and fries from Burger King. Fast food wouldn't have been her first choice, but she'd worked hard enough today to feel an ache in her shoulders and back. She wasn't in the mood for cooking.

Of all people, they encountered his friend Austin and Austin's parents at the restaurant. The two boys ate quickly and ran off to play in the pit of plastic balls, giving Erin time to ask how they liked the bigger daycare center.

Austin's mother made a face. "I still have mixed feelings. There's a kid I'd call a bully except he's maybe four years old. Austin has come home crying a few days. At least there *are* other boys his age."

"Don't forget the lice outbreak," her husband said.

"Yes! And lice seem to have defenses against the shampoo you're supposed to use, so I've had to comb and comb and comb." She wrinkled her nose. "And then they came back, either because one of the parents didn't do the job adequately or because the facility didn't clean well enough. Of course, they had to close for a couple of days while this was going on."

Austin's dad grinned at Erin. "Bet you wish you'd moved Toby sooner, huh?"

She had to laugh. "I keep going back and forth. He really misses Austin, but Mrs. Hall is so good about me dropping him for as little as an hour or two at a time. I doubt most places would permit that."

"No, I think there are strict rules about drop-offs," the boy's mother conceded. "But Austin misses Toby."

"I'll visit the place," Erin decided as the boys ran back begging for ice cream cones. Or maybe she'd just check the drop-off limitations and price on the website first. And yes, kids could pick up lice just about anywhere, but the thought made Erin shudder.

"I'll call, and we can plan for Toby to come over on a Saturday or Sunday to play," Austin's mother suggested.

The boys cheered.

On the drive home, Erin said, "Weren't we lucky to see Austin and his parents?"

"Uh-*huh*," Toby agreed. "*He* says he wishes he still went to Mrs. Hall's."

Erin wondered if that was true or whether he'd been momentarily inspired by getting to play with Toby.

"He says a boy there hits him sometimes," he added.

Erin had been keeping a sharp eye on her rearview mirror to be sure they weren't being followed, but what he'd just said had her mouth dropping open. That was more than the preschool version of bullying. How would she feel if she picked up Toby one day and saw a bruise on him courtesy of that brat?

Rationally, she knew the boy might be struggling with hard times—say, his parents had separated. But she was protective of her own son, likely because of the way Shawn had so utterly rejected him. Maybe Toby was bored at Mrs. Hall's, but he was also safe, and it wasn't as if he couldn't play with younger children, even if most of them were girls.

She made herself study her mirrors again as she turned onto their street. Home looked good right now. Thank goodness for the longer days this time of year, because it hadn't even occurred to her to leave on lights. With dusk, it was getting to be a little harder to make out details as she turned into her driveway,

Still, she didn't notice any vehicles in driveways or at the curb that didn't belong. Once she'd helped Toby out of the car, she took another careful look around, then listened as he chattered about a new game they'd played today at Mrs. Hall's. The day couldn't have been *that* dull.

Once she unlocked the front door, Toby slipped past her and ran ahead. She had barely locked up when he screamed.

ERIN HAD NEVER been so glad in her life as she was when she ran to the dining room and saw Toby alone. He wasn't hurt—*thank you, God*—and no stranger had broken in to grab him.

Only then did she let herself see what he had.

His favorite toys were sturdy plastic animals: dinosaurs, a mastodon, elephants, lions, tigers, horses, cows, whales, a hammerhead shark. They bought a new one every time they went to the Seattle zoo. He kept them in a box. Somebody had been in his bedroom, had carried his toys into the dining room, dumped them out—and methodically beheaded every one. That somebody must have used a sharp knife, she couldn't help thinking as she stared in shock.

Her antique sycamore table looked as if an ax had been taken to it.

Finally, she turned slowly to see that, just as in the garage the other night, tubs had been tossed around and dumped on top of each other, and the stuff inside had been trampled.

Terror seized her as if a real tiger strolled toward them, tail twitching, lips pulled away from its long, sharp teeth.

What if whoever had done this was still in the house?

Erin grabbed Toby by the hand, swung him to her hip and ran back the way she came. With her shaking hand, she fumbled with the lock on the door. The moment it gave way, she ran for her truck. She gave one wild glance back but saw no one pursuing, no dark shape visible through the front window. Even so, she unlocked the driver door, all but threw Toby in and clambered in after him before locking the doors again. Finally, she got the key in the ignition, started the engine with a roar and backed out into the street.

Not until they were half a block away did she brake, hearing herself whimpering, and look at her son, who watched her with shock as tears ran down his cheeks.

SAM WAS JUST thinking about leaving his house when his phone rang. *Not a call-out, please.* The lack of any decent night's sleep recently was catching up with him. He'd had to work at convincing himself to get moving for another stakeout on Erin's block. A couple of the buyers of the goods auctioned off at the storage facility hadn't had a break-in yet. Why would the guy go back to Erin's until he'd checked out other possibilities?

But Sam knew he also wouldn't be able to sleep worth a damn if he stretched out in his own bed because he'd thought, *nah, the guy won't be back yet.* Those sounded like famous last words to him.

And now Erin's name showed on the screen of his phone. "Erin?"

"Sam?" she whispered, followed by a strange sound. Her teeth chattering?

His alarm jumped into the red zone. "What happened?"

"I've been gone all day." She had obviously gathered her composure. "We…we just got home. Somebody has been in the house. He ransacked a few piles of tubs, but that's not the worst part."

The hair rose on the back of his neck. "What? What's the worst part?"

"He...he got a bunch of toys from Toby's bedroom. Animals. And he..." another chatter of teeth "...cut their heads off."

Sam swore viciously. "Are you still in the house?"

"Nuh...no. We ran out and locked ourselves in the truck. And I'm up the block where I can see the house. I don't think anyone is still there, but..."

"Okay, good. That's smart. I'm on my way." In fact, farther on his way than he'd realized. He shouldn't drive when he was oblivious to what he was doing. "Why don't you stay on the phone?"

"No, that's okay." She was calmer now. "I'm sorry I have to keep calling you like this—"

"Don't be. Haven't I made it clear that I want to hear from you if anything at all feels wrong?"

A meek "yes" tweaked something under his breastbone. What if she'd called 9-1-1 instead of his number, and he'd heard what happened tomorrow? He'd have guessed she hadn't trusted him...or maybe didn't want to bother him? He'd have felt sick about it, that's what.

It wasn't necessary, but when he reached the highway, he slapped on his flashers and accelerated. Drivers moved over to let him race by. He didn't go a lot above the speed limit but enough to cut the time it took him to get to her house by a good ten minutes.

The moment he reached her street, he searched for her truck. There it was, almost to the corner, facing her house so she could watch it. Approaching from the other direction, he swerved right into her driveway and slammed on the brakes.

Pulling his service weapon, he jumped out and ran to her front door, which stood open. He cast a glance to see that she hadn't started back to the house. Good.

"Police!" he called, shouldering the door wide enough open to let him in, then set about clearing the house. Doing that included stepping over Toby's toys, something that would make him sick once he allowed himself to take in the ugly threat aimed at a small boy and his vulnerable mother.

The kitchen window was broken, just enough to allow an arm to reach in and move the latch so the window could be opened. Things had been swept from the kitchen countertop, too, in a flash of temper: stoneware canisters that had held white flour, whole wheat flour and sugar were smashed on the floor along with a bottle of olive oil crushed by a heavy foot. The dish drainer was dumped on the floor, too, some of the dishes broken.

When had the break-in occurred? The intruder had made some noise. Had he known neighbors weren't yet home from work? Or did he not care? He seemed to lack any semblance of self-restraint, which was a big part of what scared Sam.

There was no indication that the burglar had gone into the garage. He could have looked around out there, then locked the door behind himself when he came back in, of course, but so far as Sam could tell, everything stored out there looked as it had after Erin picked up after the last intrusion.

Maybe the guy had just wanted time to look for the possessions he regarded as his in the house—but it was equally possible that terrorizing Erin had been his goal.

If so, he'd succeeded. Sam felt sick looking at those toys. He'd had plastic animals like that himself when he was a kid. So had Michael. To threaten a child to get at his mother... That struck Sam as evil, not a word he could remember using a lot.

He made a quick call for a fingerprint tech, even though he knew the intruder would have worn gloves, then put on latex gloves himself and picked up all the animals and their heads, setting them carefully in their box. He closed the lid. Out of sight, out of mind probably wouldn't work, but Toby didn't need to see this again.

Finally, he called Erin.

He went to meet them at the front door. Toby clung to her, nearly strangling her from the looks of it. Her face had a pinched look he hated to see.

"Hey," he said gently.

"How did he get in?" she asked.

"Kitchen window." He wasn't surprised she hadn't noticed. In fact, he was glad she hadn't hung around trying to figure something like that out. Getting herself and Toby out of the house had been the smartest thing she could do. "Not a big hole. We can tape some cardboard over it, but the window will have to be replaced."

"Mr. Weaver is going to start questioning whether he wants me as a tenant."

"We're having a string of unrelated break-ins in this part of the county," Sam said. "No reason he needs to know that somebody, uh—"

"Has it in for me in particular?" She shuddered, then kissed the top of her little boy's head. "Maybe if I'm lucky he'll upgrade the window from aluminum to vinyl."

She hadn't moved from the porch. He stepped back. "I

picked up the toys and put them out of sight. Have you two had dinner yet?"

"Yes, that's why we're getting home so late." She inched inside, shuffled forward a few feet, and then her dilated eyes met his. "Can you tell *when* he was here? Did he wait for us or—?"

"No indication of that." Sam didn't have to say, *No way to tell if he did.* He could have fled out the back when he heard Sam's siren. She had to know that. "I'm hoping you can tell if anything—especially an entire tub—is missing. Looks kind of different in here to me."

Her head turned as she explained what she'd done today, finding room for a significant amount of goods in her now-doubled booth at the antique mall. "That may make it harder for me to tell if something else is missing, but I'll try."

"Okay." He let them pass him and then gently herded them to the kitchen. Gaze falling on the damaged table, he immediately regretted his move, but there wasn't a lot of choice here.

Expression stricken, she said, "I'll put a tablecloth on for now." The set of her mouth firmed. "I loved this table."

Those cuts were deep. Refinishing wasn't going to save it.

"Toby?" she said. "Can I set you down?"

He shook his head hard and tightened his hold.

Sam stepped forward. "Hey, buddy," he said. "Can I hold you? Your mom needs to look around."

Toby sniffled, cast a teary-eyed look at Sam, then nodded. When Sam closed the last distance, the boy almost threw himself into Sam's arms.

Erin looked surprised but also surreptitiously rolled her shoulders. Seeing Sam's expression, she said, "I hauled a lot of stuff today. Toby weighs at least as much as the chest of drawers I carried out to my pickup."

Sam chuckled even though he didn't feel any kind of amusement. The brutal nature of this break-in on top of the last one let him feel as if he didn't dare take his eyes off Erin and Toby. No more assuming they'd be safe during the daytime. What was more, he didn't like imagining her straining to get something as sizable as a dresser out of the house and up into the bed of her truck.

"You have any help on the other end?" he asked.

"Actually, yes. Another proprietor helped carry all the heavy things in from that first load, and then I had a different assistant when I got back with the second load. I really emptied quite a bit of space here."

"Anything from the garage?"

"The dresser, a table and a lamp. Otherwise, I had things I've already researched and priced packed near the front door. I pointed out that pile to you, didn't I?"

She had.

He sat down with Toby, both of them watching as she pretended to ignore the mess on her kitchen floor and instead wandered through the dining room and living room, making little cries now and then. Sam felt sure there was some breakage, which a small entrepreneur could ill afford. That said, she had plenty of inventory. His mouth actually quirked at that thought.

Finally, she came back and sat down. "I don't know. I can't be sure."

He'd had time to think and said, "My guess is, if he found what he was looking for, he wouldn't have done this other...damage." He tipped his head toward the shards of broken canisters and dishes on the floor as well as toward the box of toys he'd shoved under the table.

Erin followed the direction of his gaze, then lifted her head to meet his eyes. "That...makes sense." She didn't move. "I need to clean up."

"I'll help," he said.

"You don't need—"

He raised his eyebrows, stopping her midsentence.

"Thank you. I feel bad. You must want to get home."

He shook his head. "No. I plan to spend the night right out front of your place. I won't be leaving you two alone again."

Although how he was supposed to accomplish that while continuing to do the rest of his job, he wasn't sure.

But then he remembered: the rookie. What was his name? Patrick... Knapstad. That was it. Young and inexperienced, but he presumably could shoot any scumbag going after Erin and Toby.

Sam guessed he ought to tell Erin about tomorrow's assistant.

Chapter Eleven

Surprised, Erin said, "Wouldn't you rather stay inside? It's not like you haven't done that before. I know the twin bed is too short for you, but…"

Even with him sitting, she was all too aware of his sheer size, both lean and muscular.

"I…didn't mean you to know I was out there." He glanced down at the boy sitting on his lap. "I don't want to put you and Toby to any trouble."

Did he *hear* himself?

Her laugh cracked in the middle. "You come running every time I call. Having Toby sleep with me is no hardship, Sam. Besides, tomorrow I can clear out the living room so you can get to the sofa, which pulls out, assuming you'd prefer that. I feel awful that because of us you can't sleep in your own bed! And that you'll be running back and forth to take care of your horses."

"They're out to pasture." He cleared his throat. "I'd be glad to stay here rather than trying to catch some sleep and keep watch at the same time in my truck."

She almost opened her mouth to ask if he really thought this faceless monster would keep coming back…but she knew better. Of course he would. The man had broken in twice already. She was grateful that she and Toby hadn't been home when he broke that window and let himself in today. What if Toby had been napping in his bedroom? How long would it have taken for her to run down the hall, rouse him, open the window, knock out the screen and climb outside?

Too long. Somebody would have been waiting for them.

She shivered at the knowledge, forcing a smile for Toby at the same time. Eyes wide, he was listening to the adults. She hoped he couldn't read between the lines. Or understand how conflicted she felt.

Depending on herself was important to Erin. She was grateful for kind gestures, like help carrying furniture or heavy boxes into the antique mall from her truck, but she hadn't had anyone to turn to in the big ways since Shawn left. And after he was gone she'd come to realize he hadn't been dependable even before that. She'd had severe morning sickness, and he hadn't changed a single behavior out of concern for her.

Water under the bridge. She shouldn't have to remind herself. Except, for Toby's sake if not her own, she couldn't afford to be too proud to accept help now.

Sam had done more for her in a week than anyone had in a long time. She couldn't let him know how attracted she was to him, or he'd assume she was just clinging out of fear and gratitude. Though, a few times there had been a glint in his eyes that made her wonder...

Well, quit, she ordered herself. If he asked her out after this was all over, that might be different.

Instinct said he wouldn't. Whether he was physically attracted to her or not, however wonderful he'd been with Toby, she couldn't imagine him choosing to get involved with a woman who had a son so close to the age his own son had been when he died. That wasn't something any parent would get over or move past. Losing Toby…

She shied away from even the thought, as if she was swerving to avoid a headlong collision on the highway. No. Just…no.

Toby wasn't the only one watching her, and she had a bad feeling Sam saw at least some of what she needed to hide.

"I'll change Toby's sheets right now," she said. "If you have anything you want to bring in…"

Sam shook his head. "I will move my truck, though. I'd rather it not be obvious you have anyone else staying here."

He was baiting a trap. Understanding what he was saying brought her fear back to the surface. "You want him to break in again."

His eyes darkened. "I do." Lines on his face deepened. "Maybe you and Toby should move to my place while I stay here. I'd like to keep you both out of this."

"This?" she repeated. "But it's all happening because of me. My decisions, what I do for a living."

He half stood, realized he didn't want to dump Toby to the floor and sat again. "You didn't do a thing to deserve being a target." That voice was unyielding. "You're making a living. The decisions on what you should bid for and what to skip, how high to go, are good ones. How could you possibly have anticipated anyone storing a petrified—" The noise he made had to be born of frustration. "I've never heard of anyone finding something like that in a storage unit. Have you?"

"No." She bit her lip. "Not paying the bill wasn't smart."

Toby had been staying unusually quiet, not surprising after discovering his beheaded toys and having her snatch him up and tear out of the house. Of course, now was the moment he asked, in his high, piercing voice, "What's petri...petrified, Mommy?"

Only from long practice was she able to smile. "Dried up." She wrinkled her nose. "You know. Like an orange that rolled to the back of the refrigerator and neither of us saw it for a long time. It would shrink and be wrinkly and hard."

Sam muffled what had to be a laugh.

"Oh," her son said. "But why would it be—?"

She cut him off. "I found something icky in one of the boxes that had been left for way too long. You don't need to know what it was. But somebody who owned the stuff in the box is mad because he forgot to pay to keep storing it, and now he wants it back. If he'd asked nicely, I might have let him take his boxes, but he's broken into our house and scared us instead. He doesn't deserve anymore for me to just say, 'Oh, that's yours? Of course you can have it.'"

Toby reached out and fingered one of the ugly gouges in the table. "I don't like him."

"I don't, either," she said. Her gaze rose almost reluctantly to meet Sam's. "We're really lucky to have Sam here so we don't have to worry so much about him, right?"

"Uh-huh." Toby had been sitting up with his back straight, but now he relaxed to rest his head against Sam's chest in a gesture of pure trust. "I like sleeping with you anyway, Mommy."

She smiled. "I know you do, pumpkin." Pretending she didn't notice the way Sam had stayed still as the little boy snuggled against him, she said, "It's time you brush your teeth, and I'll tuck you into bed before I make sure Sam has something to eat."

"We coulda brought him a hamburger and fries."

"We would have, if we'd known what we would find at

home. As it is, *we* had dinner, and Sam hasn't. And your tummy is full, so you don't have to watch Sam eat."

"But…"

She leveled a mom stare at him. Toby sighed, sat up again and slid from Sam's lap. "Will you come say g'night to me?" he asked the imposing, armed man he'd assumed would be glad to snuggle him. "When I'm ready?"

Her heart almost broke at the stunned expression on Sam's lean face.

"Yeah." He cleared his throat. "Of course I will, buddy."

SAM TRIED TO persuade Erin that she didn't need to feed him, but failed. Unlike Toby, she sat across the table from him and watched him eat a black bean quesadilla she'd put together with amazing speed. Unfortunately, she kept nibbling on her lower lip, which he found distracting.

After clearing his plate, he laid down his fork. "I think I told you earlier that I'd try to find another officer to help go through boxes."

"I remember."

Her clear gray-green eyes held as much trust as her son's bright blue ones had. That kind of trust usually was something he shied away from. A man could fail to live up to it…but he knew in his head, if not his heart, that there'd been nothing he could do to save Michael. Failing Erin and Toby wasn't an option.

"He's not going to be as much use as I'd hoped for," Sam continued. "He's young—a rookie—and wearing a cast because he broke an ankle. I didn't ask, but he's presumably on crutches." Or a walking cast? Did it matter? "Which means he can't haul the heavier stuff for you. But there'd no reason he can't go through tubs as fast as I can, and he's armed."

A flicker of worry—disappointment?—crossed her face. "Will he be here instead of you tomorrow?"

"I should be here, too, for some of the day. I get called out often, though, and I've asked to be notified every time there's a residential break-in." He frowned. "I should have mentioned the antique mall, too."

"I can ask the owner to let you know if anything like that happens."

"Okay."

"I'm sorry I didn't get more done today—"

Sam shook his head. "You can't just drop your job. I understand that. Anyway, opening some space may make our work here go faster."

She offered him a cup of coffee, which he accepted despite his intention to go to bed soon. He didn't expect to sleep deeply anyway.

Bringing a mug to the table, she asked, "Did I mention talking to Jeremy Conyers? I gather he's starting to go through records stored in his uncle's garage?"

"So he tells me. Did he call you?"

"No, I just wanted to remind him to keep an eye out for anything that might be connected to the unit that had such expensive things in it." She mentioned the letters, which didn't sound all that helpful to Sam, but alarmed him in a different way.

"I'd rather you let up for now on trying to find these people," he said. "Probably that box wasn't connected to them, but I've started to wonder whether the guy really had an entire unit filled with his own possessions. What if someone in his family said, 'Sure, you're welcome to store what you need to in our rental'?"

"That would explain why he didn't know the rent wasn't being paid anymore," she said slowly.

"Exactly."

She made a face. "Okay. It's not like tracking those people down is a high priority anyway."

He should have gulped instead of sipped his coffee, then suggest she start for bed while he moved his truck. The need to stretch out in bed was creeping up on him anyway, but mostly he was disturbed by how comfortable he felt in one way with this woman…and how on edge he felt in another way.

He hadn't let himself feel much for anyone in a long time. He'd been conscious that even with close friends, some space had opened to separate them. His grief hadn't let him forge new connections. As for women, he'd gone out a few times and slept with one, but afterward he didn't like himself much. He hadn't especially liked *her*, and going through the mechanics without emotion wasn't him. It never had been, but now, he was best off to keep to himself.

Except, where Erin was concerned, he was having some trouble convincing himself he should. For the first time in a long while, he'd reacted immediately—to her curves, to her fine-boned face and to her courage. That physical attraction had deepened as he found her to be generous, determined, fiercely protective of her boy…and tender. Sam was shocked by how much he wanted some of that for himself.

He let them fall into general conversation that smacked of first-date exchanges. She was so hopelessly behind on what movies were coming out in the theater and streaming, she hardly remembered what she'd liked. Her work and

Toby consumed her time. She didn't say a lot about the ex, but Sam already had developed a serious case of hate where he was concerned. Not that it mattered, since she hadn't so much as set eyes on the guy since he'd walked out on her.

"FedEx brought the divorce papers. I signed them and sent them back." She shrugged as if there was no emotional hit anymore to something that had to have been part of the kind of betrayal you never let go of.

He admitted he hadn't been to a movie theater in years but refrained from stating he didn't date. He did watch an occasional show streaming but read more often than he turned on his television.

His mouth quirked. "Except for sports. I follow professional football and especially baseball. I played all the way through college, then in a minor league for a couple years before hanging it up to became a cop."

"Really?" She looked fascinated. "You played professional baseball?"

He laughed. "If you can call it that when the pay is so pitiful, the crowds so small and the amenities so pathetic. If my wife hadn't worked, too—" Whoa! What was he thinking?

"I'll bet she didn't mind. I mean, pro sports always sound glamorous."

He'd walked right into that one. "Yeah. She had a lot more faith than I did that I'd get called up and that fame and fortune would be ours. Truth is, I'd started having shoulder pain before I even signed on, and it got worse for all that I tried to ignore it." He grimaced. "A lot of my teammates were younger—they'd been signed out of high school—and I began to feel like an old man. Got bored, too."

Her head tipped a little as she studied him. "So you

didn't quit after a serious injury. Or did you wait until the end of the season?"

"Nope. Threw a pitch in practice, felt grinding pain and walked off the mound. Told the manager I was done, went straight to the locker room—which, by the way, wasn't half as nice as the one at my high school—got dressed and went home."

Where he'd been making dinner when Ashley walked in.

"I hope your wife was supportive." Erin made a face. "I shouldn't have said that. It's none of my business."

"Well, you know the outcome." Something he hadn't shared with anyone in years, even though a few people he worked with knew what had happened. "She threw something at me to express her fury, wanted to know why I hadn't asked her opinion and went out and got drunk with a girlfriend. After that, she started keeping the makings for her favorite drinks on hand."

"You must have been young when you had your son."

"Too young," he said bluntly, "except I fell in love with him in a way I didn't know was possible."

She touched the back of his hand, fingertips gentle. "I know."

Sam knew she did. He saw it on her face every time she looked at Toby. Sam didn't doubt that Ashley had loved Michael, too, but...not the same way. Maybe amid her dreams of that glamorous future, she'd just been too young to commit so intensely to a child who consumed a lot of energy and time.

"Yeah." He heard his own gruffness. "I should move that truck and let you go to bed."

To his regret, Erin snatched her hand back. "You're right.

Here I am being nosy when you're just thinking about doing your job."

"No."

In the act of pushing back her chair, she went still. Her eyes searched his.

"You have to know—" His throat felt like it was full of gravel, and his voice sounded as if it was, too. Somehow he was standing.

"Know what?" she whispered, rising to her feet.

"You're more than a job." Oh, that was eloquent.

Eyes wide, she waited.

"I'd like to kiss you."

Her eyes dilated, and she moistened her lips. "I'd like that. Although…"

"Although?"

"I… It's been a long time. I mean…" She gave a funny, one-shoulder shrug. "Except for Toby."

"I haven't been involved with anyone for a while, either." He might have smiled; he wasn't sure. "I think I remember how to do it."

Erin laughed, which gave him a major bump in his mood and enough impetus to walk around the table, slide a hand around the nape of her neck and drink in the details that made up a face he'd been drawn to at first sight. Then he bent his head and kissed her.

Chapter Twelve

Erin's last thought was, *What if I've forgotten what to do?*

His lips were so gentle, she quit thinking at all, just savored. And then they firmed, which was even better, and he nibbled at her lower lip until she did the same to his. Of course, that let him in, and the slide of his tongue against hers had to be the most erotic thing she'd felt in forever.

She gripped his shirt in both hands and just held on as the kiss deepened, still at an almost leisurely pace. His hand cupped the back of her head now, tilting it to give him the best access. She wanted more and got it when he wrapped his arm around her and pulled her tight against him. Nothing had ever felt better in her life than that long, hard body. She rose on tiptoe, loving the sensations from rubbing against him. She wanted to climb him, discover the warmth of his skin. Maybe this was all instinct. If so, hers was on target.

Sam groaned, freed his mouth from hers to nip her jawline and then her neck. She let her head fall back as he kissed his way down her throat to the hollow at the base, where he startled her with a hot, damp touch of his tongue.

When she jerked in reaction, he lifted his head. His eyes were darker than she'd ever seen them, but blazing, too, if that wasn't a contradiction.

Erin wasn't sure she even breathed as they stared at each other.

Another raw sound escaped him, and he stepped away. Without his support, she swayed before she grabbed the back of a chair to steady herself.

"I didn't mean to take it that far," he said roughly.

"I…" She knew she blinked a couple of times. "I liked it." So dignified: she'd just bared herself!

Only he grinned. "I did, too. We'll have to do it again."

Now would be good.

But he was rolling those broad shoulders and moving his head as if to ease tension in it.

Had he worried that Toby might still be awake? And… she wasn't ready to invite Sam into her bed, was she? She didn't groan, but only because she restrained herself. If he'd kept kissing her like that, she doubted she would've ever paused for a moment of calm decision. As it was, Toby was asleep in her bed, the only one large enough for her and Sam to share. Although they could surely manage on a twin bed…

If her cheeks weren't already red, they must be now from the heat burning her face.

Sam cupped her chin, which rested nicely in his broad palm. His expression was regretful, but even as she gazed up at him, he donned his usual calm mask. Becoming the cop again, because that was what he thought he needed to do? Or stepping back, figuratively if not literally, because he wasn't sure he should have kissed her?

All she could do was rub her cheek against his hand, smile and step back in actuality.

"I should have moved my truck sooner," he said. "There's still enough traffic out there, he's unlikely to be hanging around now. It won't take me long, but you don't have to wait up for me. I'll lock the door behind myself if you want to start getting ready for bed."

However tactfully he'd phrased it—that was an order. He'd prefer she had used the bathroom and disappeared into her bedroom before he returned. That stung, but she had too much pride to let him see that.

"Go," she said, flapping her hand. "Fair warning, Toby is an early riser, which means I am, too."

"I did notice last time. That's fine. Knapstad may be here as early as eight."

She wished him good-night and headed for the hall. Only a minute later, she heard the quiet sound of the front door closing.

THE THUNDER OF small footsteps in the hall brought Sam lurching out of a dream he hadn't been enjoying.

"Mommy!" was followed by a "shh" that came way too late.

Sam groaned, yanked the pillow out from under his head and slapped it over his face. No, he hadn't slept well, for multiple reasons. Nothing like staying alert for any faint sound that didn't belong—a sound made by a killer—along with brooding over a kiss that had been even better than he had imagined...but that also scared him. The happy boy out in the hall being one reason for that.

No clock. He groped blindly for his phone lying on a headboard shelf. It read 6:03 a.m. Glad the pillow would muffle the sound, he groaned again. He'd give a lot for another hour.

Mother and son had moved out to the kitchen. He heard a chair scraping, Toby chattering, the refrigerator door opening and closing. Man, he hoped she didn't mind him using her shower. And that she didn't have a low-flow showerhead.

He emerged twenty minutes later, wishing he'd brought a change of clothes but figuring no one on the job would notice, given that he wore similar getups most days. If his day included an appearance in court, he'd have had to run home, but as it was, he could do that later. Pack a duffel bag, he decided, even if he would still have to go back and forth to take care of the horses.

When he appeared in the kitchen, Erin smiled at him without quite meeting his eyes. Toby beamed, and Sam couldn't resist stopping to ruffle the boy's hair.

"Just in time for breakfast," Erin said and set a big bowl filled with scrambled eggs on the table to join a pile of toast and a plate heaped with bacon. He had to guess this breakfast was much bigger than what she and Toby usually ate.

He pulled out a chair. "This looks amazing. If you went to a lot of extra effort just for me, though—"

"No, Toby and I like to treat ourselves at least once a week. And I'm guessing a bowl of cereal wouldn't hold you long."

No, it wouldn't, but he said, "I don't like adding to your workload."

"I love bacon," she assured him and sat at the third place.

A red-and-white-checked tablecloth covered the deep slices in the wood. Would Toby forget they were there? Sam wondered if any of the tables she had out in the garage would end up here as replacement. Or maybe she'd wait until she saw something she liked better.

He ate with pleasure, even as he watched Erin alternating a bite for herself with tucking a napkin in the neck of Toby's T-shirt, steadying the glass of orange juice that he had to clutch in both hands to get to his mouth, wiping up spills and so on. The familiarity of it felt… Sam couldn't quite decide. He liked seeing Erin helping the little boy without ever getting irritated or making him feel less than capable. The deep ache beneath his breastbone wasn't unexpected. Weirdly, though, Toby reminded Sam of Michael less and less often.

Michael had been quieter and more reserved, even as a toddler. Sam had sometimes worried that Ashley ignored him or grew impatient with him. In the first couple of years he didn't really see that—but he was away a lot, traveling with the team. Later, once Ashley began to drink at home even during the day—

He told himself to knock it off. Why rewind a video that couldn't be edited?

Toby finished eating first, of course, and announced he wanted to play. Only then he said, sadly, "I wish I could play with my animals."

"We'll buy new ones," Erin assured him. "You have plenty of other toys. Why don't you do a puzzle?"

Sam thought he had a box of similar animals up in his attic. Some had been his as a kid. Of course, they'd gone with Michael when Ashley left Sam, but after the accident—

More he didn't want to think about, but the memory of packing everything that had been Michael's flashed whether Sam liked it or not. He'd left Ashley's clothes, jewelry and even the furniture in the small apartment for her mother to deal with. Everything of Michael's, he'd taken, even though his grandmother had loved her grandson.

Why not climb up in the attic later, when he was home? What had he been saving them for? If Michael could know, he'd be glad his favorite toys would be loved.

A sound escaped Sam that he hoped neither Erin nor Toby heard. He rarely let himself get morose. Give the toys to another boy who'd enjoy them. Nothing complicated about that.

He finished eating, thanked Erin again and set to work. Struggling with his focus, he'd gone through four plastic tubs in the living room before a vehicle pulled into the driveway beside Erin's truck. He waved her back to a seat and went to the door to allow the rookie in.

Sam immediately saw the walking cast. Good. Crutches would have gotten in the way. Knapstad was tall with a decent build and a boyish face, especially when he looked eager as he did now.

"Detective. I hope I'm not too early."

"No, we've been at work for a while." Realizing how that sounded, Sam added, "Ms. Reed has a young son who likes to get up with the chickens."

"Oh." Knapstad smiled broadly. "I'm glad to have something useful to do. They've had me planted at the front desk."

Sam introduced the deputy and Erin, then dug in his pocket for latex gloves to hand him before sitting him down with a tub. He detailed as many of the contents from the tub that contained the dried-up tongue as he could recall, hoping that gave a good idea what to watch for.

"Nothing seemed to go together," Erin said from off to the side. "Except they all belonged to women. Well, the tongue, we don't know, but—" She looked sorry she'd let herself rattle on.

"So you think—"

"Trophies," Sam said grimly. "That's our best guess. Our difficulty is that Ms. Reed has been productive lately in purchasing contents of storage units that came up for auction." He paused to let her explain why that was and what she did with the things she bought, then continued, "That means she has more here than usual, and because the house and garage are crowded, the contents of any particular unit didn't end up together. A tub might have been shoved in anywhere it fit."

The rookie was looking around in a certain amount of awe and probably bemusement.

"We can't assume any others from the same unit were the same color or even a plastic tub versus a cardboard box or—" Sam had noted a few stuffed black plastic bags out in the garage "—a sack."

"Sad to say, that's true." Erin smiled at the deputy. "Sam—er, the detective or I will keep dragging boxes over for you to go through. With a lot of them, it's often clear that it's not what we're looking for. You may find ones full of dishes wrapped in newspapers, or pots and pans. Sometimes clothes, but that's less common."

"Because people don't put their clothes in storage."

"Right. They put furniture, knickknacks, toys their kids have outgrown, washers and dryers—" for some reason she made a face at that "—photo albums, books, CDs, framed art. Well, you'll see."

She got Knapstad started, asking him to let her know if he saw anything he suspected was especially valuable or at least easily salable so she could tag that box, then resumed her original spot.

Sam continued with the box he'd been going through— clothes and shoes, but a man's. He continued carefully, just in case their possible serial killer was an equal opportunity offender and had murdered a man or two along the way. When he was done, he said, "I'd recommend thrift store," and took a sticky note and marker from her to affix to the outside.

They had a system now: stuff that looked good for the booth at the mall or potential eBay in one pile, thrift store in another, uncertain or mixed in yet another pile. Because of the room she'd opened up yesterday, they were able to slide boxes around instead of having to wedge them back where they'd come from so as to be able to pull out another one.

Toby popped out every fifteen minutes or so and either watched them or wanted Mommy. She disappeared with him briefly, her eyes always meeting Sam's when she returned. He knew why; she was asking, *Did you find anything?*

He hoped if there was anything else gruesome to be found, it was in one of his boxes, not hers. Every time, he gave a slight shake of his head.

He couldn't say he minded when at about ten o'clock his phone rang. He knew the number: the lab where he'd delivered the tub with everything *but* the tongue.

Sam took his phone out to the porch before he answered the call.

It was the same woman he'd spoken to that day. Her eagerness raised the hair on the back of his neck. "We have hits on several fingerprints on items in that tub you brought us. The outside of it, the lid inside and out, had prints we're assuming belonged to one individual. We found the same fingerprints on items in the box, but also separate prints, not surprisingly."

His heartbeat had quickened. Was it possible it would be this easy?

"Names?" he asked.

"Only forensic hits for the ones on the tub and lid," she

said regretfully. "Three of the other prints belong to murder victims."

It was like a gut punch. They'd been right.

"I assume you have contact info for investigators?"

"I do. I'm sure you're not surprised to hear that the ones on the tub are associated with those three crimes…and have shown up at other scenes where the victim was never found or where the fingerprints were assumed to have belonged to a friend or someone else who'd had reason to be in the home or car."

"Why don't I come in?" he said. "That way I can see which fingerprints go with what. Oh—did you hear from the ME? I assume he came up with DNA?"

"He did and sent it off, but reminded me how long it would likely be before we get a response. That said—" her voice brightened "—now we have good reason to put a rush on it."

"We do indeed. The offender is right here, searching desperately for his goodies."

"And may have his eye on another victim," she added quietly.

Not a thought he liked. Especially since he knew what woman this piece of scum was watching.

SAM HAD GIVEN Erin his okay to go to the antique mall the following day. Call it a hall pass, she thought, her nose wrinkling…except she didn't actually mind his protectiveness.

She was even more frightened now and could tell that he was, too. He didn't like to let her out of his sight. She didn't love going out on her own, either, but Marsha had called to ask her to come by since a gentleman—that was the word she used—had been asking questions about items she had for sale.

In barely more than twenty-four hours, quite a few things from Erin's double booth had already sold, too, so Sam helped her load the bed of her truck before he took off in response to a call about a break-in that he didn't think was linked to the storage facility.

Usually she would have taken Toby with her, but the tension had risen to a point where she felt better having him at Mrs. Hall's for the day. If only she had family she could place him with! Hearing verification that the box had, just as Sam guessed, held trophies from multiple murders had shaken her world. She'd have been shocked to see a mugging; the odds of finding something like this were infinitesimal.

But she didn't know how to do anything but go on.

After dropping off Toby and driving to the mall, she carried a box of miscellaneous items she'd priced some time ago in through the back door. A woman browsed in her booth, smiled vaguely at her but otherwise paid no attention as Erin set down the tub, peeled off the lid and looked around to see where she had gaps that needed filling. The only other person close by was a man hovering in a booth across the aisle, which specialized in antique tools, but he didn't seem interested in them or her. She guessed he might be the woman's husband, bored but trying to entertain himself.

Once she had a better idea what she needed, she let herself out the back again, greeting the proprietor of another booth getting out of her truck even before the door swung shut. Erin pushed it open again, blocked it with a brick they frequently used for the purpose, and they went in together carrying their next load.

By the time Erin had restocked her enlarged area, she was wondering about the man who had been so insistent she come by to talk to him. Well, she needed to see Marsha anyway. She finished stacking several now-empty plastic tubs and was straightening when she almost bumped into someone.

She felt a flare of alarm when she recognized the man she'd noticed earlier. Apparently, not a bored husband. Had he been watching her the entire time? Waiting until she was alone?

She'd like to believe he was only being considerate by waiting until she was free, but he didn't back away when she nearly bumped into him. He leaned toward her, his expression so intense *she* wanted to retreat from him.

Her voice squeaking the tiniest bit, she asked, "May I help you?" She was already cataloguing her impressions. Midthirties to early forties, she guessed, seeing a little gray in the afternoon stubble on his jaw. Brown hair, gray eyes that glittered, a mouth compressed into a thin line and a solid build. Cords stood out in his arms, bared by a V-necked white T-shirt…and his fingers were curled into something close to fists. Several pockets of his cargo pants bulged with unknown items.

"Yeah." He seemed to bite off the word. "What took you so long?"

"I'm not here most of the time. The ladies at the counter in front could have helped you. Anyway, I've been here for probably half an hour. I wouldn't have minded talking as I worked." She sneaked a peek one way, then the other. Was it bad luck that nobody happened to be in sight?

"Where do you get this stuff?" He jerked his head toward a glass-fronted cabinet.

She frequently used that word herself, but his tone belittled her work. Taking a casual step away from him, she said, "Oh, a variety of places. Garage sales—most weekends, I go to any in the area." Except, when had she last been to one? "Even thrift stores, occasionally. When the contents of a storage unit become available because the owner quit paying the rent, I sometimes bid to purchase them. If you're interested in something in particular and care where it came from, I can try to remember."

"That." He pointed at a cut-glass vase.

She frowned at it, finally shaking her head. "I'm afraid I don't recall. I frequently have cut-glass vases and plates. If you're looking for one—"

"What about *that*?" he snapped, this time stabbing his finger toward an unusual pair of wrought-iron bookends.

"I—" She started to shake her head, even though she could picture the plastic tub they had been in.

"You don't know." He sneered. "What kind of business is this, when you don't know anything about this junk you're selling?"

Her temper began to simmer. "I know quite a lot about everything I sell," she snapped in turn. "I research every item, then determine how old it may be and a reasonable value for it." She took offers on occasion, but not one from this guy, if driving down her price was his goal. "If you disagree with my asking price, there are at least forty other booths in this antique mall alone. Feel free to look elsewhere."

"I don't want to look elsewhere. I want to know where you get your things and what else you have that isn't displayed yet."

He was giving her the creeps. Her gaze drifted down to his work boots. Yes, those would be good for trampling.

It occurred to her to try to place him into the frame where the masked man fit who'd beaten Jeremy and lit the fire. She couldn't be sure, but...he was around the same size and bulk.

A ball formed in her stomach, and her instinct begged her to run. Instead, she squared her shoulders. "You're making me uncomfortable. I do have other stock in storage. If you're looking for one thing in particular, ask. Otherwise, you're welcome to browse, but I need to leave."

He took a long stride closer to her. "You're not much on customer service, are you?"

Nerves prickled beneath her skin. "Excuse me."

He grabbed her arm at the same moment voices cut into the bubble they seemed to have occupied.

"Yes, one of our booths has a wonderful collection of vintage quilts and other fabric arts." It was Marsha, and she was in this aisle.

The rumble of a male voice answered, followed by the more excitable voice of a woman.

The hostile man took his hand from Erin's arm and backed away. "I'll be back," he said, low and rough, before he turned and rushed away just before the other three people came in sight.

Shaking, Erin's first thought was to call Sam. Her heart hammered, and she gave herself a minute to calm down. She could be overreacting. They all got unpleasant customers.

She wanted to think he'd left...but she'd find someone to walk her out to her truck to be sure she wasn't alone in the parking lot—and that nobody followed her.

Chapter Thirteen

Sam stayed at his desk at headquarters to make his calls, received with intense interest and cooperation by every investigator he reached. The crimes had occurred over four years, not so long that a detective would have forgotten one that had remained unsolved.

The picture that began to form for Sam was even worse than he'd expected. The crimes linked to the man's fingerprints started with brutal rapes and escalated into rapes followed by murders. The women were in their twenties to early thirties, all pretty, blond to mid-range brown hair. One had been a graduate student at the University of Washington; another an attorney; and a third in sales at Nordstrom. Two had been attacked in their own homes, others snatched somewhere between work or a social engagement and home. Every detective to whom Sam spoke wanted this guy with anger he shared.

The earliest crime, a rape, had happened in Bend, Oregon. That woman had been a ski instructor and lift operator at Bachelor Butte. The first murder the fingerprints pinpointed was in Beaverton, a suburb of Portland, Oregon. The other crimes had been committed in the greater Seattle area, not surprisingly, since the killer's trophy stash had been deposited in a storage unit in Snohomish County, just to the north of King County, which included Seattle.

Neither rape victim that survived had recognized their attacker, because he had never removed the black ski mask he wore over his head, and he'd also battered their faces to the point where their eyes had swollen shut. The closest any of them had to a witness was a woman who had seen a pickup truck pull to the shoulder of a rural road. The driver had gotten out and dragged something out of the bed of his truck and tossed it in the ditch. The woman had been too far away, given the darkness, to make out the license plate or see any more than to believe he wore something black over his head. A hood, she'd assumed at the time. She waited until he was gone before she ran to see what he'd dumped.

She admitted to screaming all the way back to her rural home and locking all the doors and windows before she called 9-1-1.

Some of the women had had an uneasy feeling they were being followed before the assaults. One victim, eventually murdered, had told a friend she'd swear someone had been in her house…but whatever made her uneasy was subliminal. She couldn't say, *That's gone*, or even, *I could tell someone looked through my drawers*.

Investigators looked hard at men in the women's lives: recent dates, boyfriends, coworkers, anyone with whom the women had clashed. They had names—but no two investigators had so much as glanced at an individual who had also come to the attention of a detective looking at another crime. Now, with what Sam was able to tell them, they were all able to eliminate everyone who'd drawn their attention.

"He's a ghost," an older detective said wearily. "Doesn't this guy have to make a living? If he's moving around the

Northwest, he sure isn't holding down a job." He paused. "Unless—"

Sam had the same thought. Their perpetrator could be a long-haul trucker, a salesman with a route, who knew? He frowned and made a note to look at what had been happening in each city leading up to the murders. There could have been conferences, fairs, art exhibits. The guy could be a runner who traveled to compete in marathons or even just ten Ks. The possibilities went on and on. Wouldn't another investigator have had the same idea? And reality was, this guy had been lurking in Sam's corner of the county for a couple weeks now.

Because this was home? Or was he renting a place locally because he was determined to recover his trophies? Probably not staying in a hotel or B & B—his comings and goings late at night would stand out, especially if he assaulted another woman and ended up with her blood on him. Everett was a big enough city to have some Airbnb rentals, but Sam doubted the smaller towns like Sultan and Monroe offered much like that. Still, it was an avenue to pursue.

Whether this was the killer's home territory or not, he'd learned that a storage unit he considered his personal vault had been violated and the contents sold off. Had he driven in and found the lock had been replaced—or there was no lock at all, and the unit was vacant? A question to ask Conyers: once the contents of a unit were auctioned, would the code to the gate still have been valid?

If the footage of traffic in and out of the facility had survived the fire, it might be worth taking the time to watch. If someone remained conscious at all times of where cameras were placed, he could keep his face from being seen, but would he bother when he'd come and gone from this facility multiple times in the past?

No matter what, everything had changed for the man now. Rage drove him, rather than his more usual targeting of a particular woman. Unless, of course, he had a dual interest in Erin.

Sam's jaw clenched so hard, his molars ached. He wanted to believe the killer had zeroed in on her house because she was one of the names Jeremy Conyers had thrown out as a possible purchaser of the contents of that particular unit, not because he'd ever set eyes on her.

Sam didn't dare let himself believe that. He thought it was irrelevant anyway. The level of rage and violence demonstrated when that scum attacked Conyers said no one who might be in his path was safe. Beheading a little kid's toy animals? That was sick. Only a monster would do that.

He'd ignored several calls for the past couple of hours, only checking messages now and again, but when Erin's number came up, he answered.

"I hope I'm not interrupting anything important," she said, sounding anxious.

Going for calm reassurance and hoping his fear wasn't leaking into his voice, he said, "No. Right now is good to talk."

"Oh. Well, I thought about calling you earlier, but I didn't want to overreact and waste your time, only I talked to Patrick—you know, Deputy Knapstad—and *he* thought I should let you know about this guy—"

Sam was still tracking her run-on sentence but thought it was time to interrupt, if only so she could catch a breath. "I want you to call me *any* time something worries you."

"Oh." She was quiet for a moment. "You know I went to the mall because a man had some questions for me."

Sam leaned forward, tension crawling up his neck. "And?"

She told him about a strange encounter with a man who hadn't fit any definition of a customer. No, Sam didn't like anything she told him.

"I don't want you there alone again," he said flatly.

"He was really creepy," Erin admitted. "But if he attacked Jeremy and is the one who broke into my house a couple of times, why would he get in my face like that? It doesn't make *sense* that he'd let me see him! What could he possibly have hoped to learn from asking me the questions he did?"

"I don't know. Maybe that vase he asked about came from one of his boxes, or he thought it might have? Or something else?"

"But if he wasn't sure about them—"

"Could he have believed he might be able to intimidate you into letting him in your house to look around?"

"Would any woman in her right mind agree to that?" Erin sounded more spirited now. "Anyway, if that's what he wanted, he'd have gotten further by being nice and interested in what I did and how I picked out what to display in the mall."

All true, but unlike some serial rapists and murderers, he might be antisocial and lack any semblance of charm. He also might be oblivious to how he presented to other people.

"Only…" Erin's tone shifted. "Did I say he grabbed me?"

"He *what*?" Sam shot to his feet. "Did he hurt you?"

"I…may have bruises. He just grabbed my arm, but—"

There was a pause. "Ugh." She must have pushed up a sleeve. "I do have bruises."

"Are you with Knapstad right now?" he asked.

"Yes. Well, I'm in the kitchen, and he's in the living room, but I'm sure he can hear me."

"Toby?"

"He's...still at Mrs. Hall's."

"Okay. We'll pick him up later."

"You can tell the bruises are from fingers digging into my arm."

Sam thought a few pungent words but didn't say them. "How did you break his hold?"

"I didn't. I got lucky, because we both heard Marsha coming down the aisle with a couple to look at a booth past mine. He let go, said he'd be back and rushed away."

"Son of a—" Sam stopped himself. "He threatened you. I mean it. You're not going there alone or just with Toby again."

"You can't trail me twenty-four hours a day."

"Watch me."

"Usually the mall is busier than it was today."

Sam dug his fingers into his hair and yanked. "Tell me you didn't go out to your truck alone."

"Of course I didn't!" She sounded annoyed, understandably, considering he was questioning her common sense. "I found a man I know to walk me out. Josh is an ex-marine, and he looks like it."

"All right." Sam forced himself to take an emotional step back. "I'm heading out in a few minutes. I should be there within half an hour."

"Don't hurry if you have something else to do. Patrick *is* here."

"I'll let you know if I get delayed." Sam ended the call.

He wished Erin were a little less gutsy, less certain she could handle anything. Because now he'd seen some crime scene photos that depicted apparently strong, successful women who'd faced a monster and lost.

SHE'D SWEAR SAM had aged a decade in one day. Unless it had been happening so gradually, she hadn't noticed until he reached a tipping point.

He sat at the kitchen table with her and the young deputy, talking about two break-ins he'd just learned about. "One is in Gold Bar. It doesn't sound like it could have anything to do with our problem. The responding deputy is thinking teenagers after the usual, stuff that's easy to sell or pawn."

Patrick nodded, appearing unsurprised.

"The other one was at the home of an antique dealer. Owns one of the stores on First Street in Snohomish." He named it, and Erin nodded.

"I've never met her, but that's a great store."

"She had some stock at home. A neighbor saw a rental truck backed up to her garage and didn't think anything of it since she moved things in and out on a regular basis. In this case, it wasn't her. She admits her security is limited. Thinks the garage door could have been forced. She does buy occasionally from auctions at storage units, but she says it's been awhile." His mouth tightened. "I called Conyers. He didn't recognize her name."

"But somebody might have told this guy that she was a dealer, so he took a look," Patrick suggested.

"That's what I'm thinking." Sam made an odd, rough sound. "I also wonder if we should warn anyone in the area who deals in vintage or antiques. Do you know how many there are?"

Erin understood his dismay. Snohomish was famous for its antique stores coupled with cafés and bakeries. Highway 2 was heavily traveled because of the ski area at the pass and because it continued into eastern Washington. Every small town along the way, including Startup, Gold Bar and Skykomish, had antique stores. And that didn't include the proprietors that clustered together in malls, like the one where she had her booth. They were talking about a staggering number of people. And what could they do to protect themselves anyway?

"But there are a couple of names Jeremy gave you that haven't had break-ins yet," she protested. "Wouldn't they make more sense?"

"Yeah. I think I need to call Ms. Cavender and—who's the other guy?"

"Walt Smith." Erin heard how stifled she sounded. The memory was all too vivid, hearing Jeremy choking out names in the hope he'd survive.

"Right. That's it." Sam rubbed his eyes. "I'll call them both this evening."

She thought he might be done, but instead he said, "Normally I wouldn't share this much detail with you, Erin, but you've already guessed at how bad your discovery was." He went on to talk about what he'd learned today, glancing rarely at the young deputy, mostly watching her. Did he fear he was terrifying her?

Well, he was, but she needed to know what she'd accidentally stumbled into. Who had been less than ten feet away from her and Toby as he battered Jeremy and then trashed and set fire to the office. Who had now broken into her house twice.

So yes, she shuddered but insisted he continue when he broke off.

Finally she asked, "Do you think these are all the women he's attacked?"

"No." Expression grim, Sam said, "I'm guessing he's worn gloves some of the time. Rape survivors don't all report the assaults. There could be women found dumped in a ditch, like the one was, with nothing to tie the body to him. Especially if he also goes for women who live on the fringe of society—prostitutes, teenage runaways—and women who are loners enough that nobody notices when they disappear. He could have left plenty more victims in his wake. That—" his gaze never wavered "—is one reason we need to find the rest of his stash."

"Are we sure—?" Patrick started to ask, but Sam cut him off.

"He doesn't know we found the one box, but what are the odds that was the only one? Did I mention that his fingerprints showed up a few places where there were break-ins but no apparent victim? Or in one case, a woman went missing and has never been located?" Voice as hard and as gritty as granite, Sam said, "We want to nail this guy for *every* woman he terrorized."

Patrick's head bobbed, as Erin was sure hers was, too.

Sam gave himself a shake. "Patrick, why don't you call it a day? We'll see you first thing in the morning. I can make calls from here this evening. I'll be staying nights until we catch this—" He swallowed whatever language he'd started to use.

"I can keep going if you need me," Patrick offered.

Erin managed a smile for him. "My eyes have started crossing, and it must be worse for you when you're not as familiar with what you're looking at. We made real progress today."

They had worked through everything in the living and dining rooms. Tomorrow, they'd start on the garage, the mere thought of which made her want to groan. If only they knew how long ago she'd won the bid on the contents of the one unit! Unfortunately, she'd started spilling over into the living room and the dining room as much as four months ago. Chagrined, she tried to remember. Could it have been longer?

She stayed sitting where she was, hands folded on the tabletop, while Sam walked Patrick out. Because he wanted to share information out of her hearing? Or was he going to collect something from his truck? She had zero interest in moving or thinking about what she could make for dinner or even about fetching Toby.

Her gaze strayed to the clock on the stove. It wasn't even quite four o'clock, nowhere near as late as she'd thought.

Sam walked back into the kitchen without her even having noticed the sound of the front door closing. Erin slowly lifted her head, to find his gaze locked onto her face. His brown eyes weren't warm, they were tumultuous. He chose the chair kitty-corner from hers, then held out his hand. After a moment, she laid her smaller hand in his.

Neither moved until he swore, half stood and pulled her to her feet.

Far from resisting, Erin all but threw herself into his arms, plastering herself against that tall, muscular body. This was what she'd needed as she sat there like a stone, trying to make sense of the violence and threats in a life that had been *peaceful*. Now…oh, she felt too much.

"I needed this," Sam growled against the top of her head. "Just let me hold you."

That wasn't all he wanted. His erection pressed against her belly, firing the nerve ends from her toes to her fingers. It was as if having him would solve everything.

She lifted her head so she could look into his eyes. "Will you…will you kiss me?"

"GOD, YES!"

Stress and fear drove him, part of the brew that made this courageous woman more desirable than anyone he'd ever met. If there weren't so much more mixed in, he'd have tried to make himself back off. But the truth was, he'd wanted her from that first interview.

His mouth closed over hers, the kiss moving past gentle and exploratory to urgent, even desperate, with warp speed. He needed her, and he needed this.

Sam discovered he'd already yanked off her shirt, leaving her hair wildly disheveled—or maybe he'd done that with his hands—and he was fighting with her bra clasp even though they still stood beside the kitchen table.

She'd asked him to kiss her, not strip her and lay her back on the table so he could bury himself in her.

"Erin," he said hoarsely.

She blinked. "Sam?"

"I want you. If you're not ready to go there, we need to bring this to a stop."

More blinks. Her cheeks were rosy, her lips plump, her usually clear gray-green eyes dark.

The wait for her to absorb what he'd said was tortuous.

"I'm ready."

It took him a second, no more. Then he groaned, captured her mouth again and picked her up to stumble blindly down the hall to her bedroom.

There, he got a grip on his hunger. She hadn't gotten close to a man since her scumbag ex had dumped her along with his smart, loving boy. Patience was needed here.

And so he laid her on the bed, kissing, touching, exploring, even as he finished peeling off her clothes. He talked, although he had no idea what he was saying. She was exquisite, long-legged, athletic yet curvy. He kissed and licked and sucked her beautiful, generous breasts with taut nipples.

He paused now and again when she tugged at his clothes. Unlacing his boots was a chore he could have lived without. At last she could explore him, too, the way she so obviously wanted to.

Stroking her wet passage, he moved between her thighs. The first pressure felt better than anything he could remember. It also wrenched him back to awareness.

"Erin." Voice guttural, he was thankful that he could still form words. "Are you on birth control?"

"No! Oh, we can't stop!"

He rested his forehead against hers and took a couple of deep breaths. "I have something. Just…give me a minute."

Sam hadn't thought they'd get here, but impulse had grabbed him after he filled up with gas a couple of days ago. He'd stuck two of the condoms in his wallet. Which was…in the pocket of his pants, wherever they were… His head turned. Tossed too far away.

But he lifted himself, made it across the room and secured the condoms. He tore one open and donned it one-handed before he reached the bed.

Erin, he found, had pushed herself up and was surveying his naked body with clear pleasure. He grinned, enjoying her blush, before sprawling half beside her, half on top of her, and kissing her until she spread her legs and her hips began moving. Finally, he pushed inside her, bearing his weight on his forearm while gripping her hip to position her.

In mere minutes, they found a rhythm as if they'd done this a thousand times. She made incoherent sounds, dug her fingers into his back and finally cried his name in seeming astonishment.

Only then did he let himself go.

Chapter Fourteen

Erin couldn't understand why she didn't feel more awkward in the aftermath of the most astonishing lovemaking she'd ever experienced. Except really, she didn't have *time*. The deadline for picking up Toby at Mrs. Hall's loomed too close. She had to hustle to get dressed, splash cold water on her face in hopes of countering the glow-in-the-dark pink accented by what might be friction burns from Sam's stubble. Hair combed…check.

Sam insisted on driving her. "Your place should be okay," he said, as if she'd argued. "Plenty of people coming and going."

He was right; she lifted her hand to greet Darren who appeared to be coming home from work.

Appearing preoccupied, Sam didn't say a word until they were almost to the babysitter's, although she saw his gaze flicking to the side mirror and back to the windshield.

"Let's eat out," he said suddenly.

"What?"

"We need the time-out," he surprised her by saying.

From the constant stress? Or did he want to put off any private talk? But she only nodded. If she'd had dinner planned, she couldn't remember what she'd had in mind.

Toby was delighted to see Sam and was chatty enough

to cover any tension between his mother and the detective. Assuming there was any, she thought in chagrin; for all she knew, Sam thought they'd had a good time that he hoped they might repeat someday if the opportunity arose.

She, on the other hand, lacked any semblance of sophistication. She'd slept with only two other men before, her high school boyfriend and Shawn. And truthfully, her own emotions were muddled. She knew that Sam had had mixed feelings about her from the beginning, if only because of Toby.

Despite all that, she enjoyed dinner at the pizza parlor, especially watching Sam continue to charm her son in a relaxed way that betrayed none of his initial discomfort.

She shouldn't have been surprised to feel her muscles tightening the minute she pulled into her driveway. Lights showed through the front window. Had she left those on? She wished she'd approached from the other direction so she could have seen the side door and window into the garage.

Sam gave her a swift look even as he leaned back to unbuckle Toby's seat belt. Then he murmured, "Why don't you let me have your keys?"

"Sure." She handed them over with relief.

By the time she helped Toby hop like a rabbit out of the truck and followed, Sam had disappeared inside. He was just coming back in from the garage when she lifted Toby to her hip and stepped inside.

He gave a slight shake of the head along with a smile, and she puffed out a breath she hadn't known she was holding.

Toby struggled to be let down. "Didn't you hear me, Mommy? Huh?"

"I'm sorry!" Her laugh seemed to fool him, at least. She smacked a kiss on the top of his head before setting him down on his feet. And what did he do but run to Sam, renewing her newest anxiety: was he getting too attached to a man who hadn't promised anything but to protect them in the short term?

She played a few games with Toby, who was disappointed because Sam excused himself to return phone calls. Then she supervised bath time and read a couple of stories to her clean, contented little boy as he snuggled beneath his covers and tried to hold out against the sleepiness that finally overcame him.

When she returned to the kitchen, Sam sat at the table. He was in the act of stretching his arms over his head until she'd swear she heard some popping sounds. Groaning, he lowered his arms before rolling his head one way, then the other. Erin had already known she wasn't the only one feeling tension, but now, with him not having noticed her in the hallway, she saw lines on his forehead she'd swear hadn't been there before.

"Is something wrong?" she asked tentatively.

He made an effort to smooth his expression that wasn't entirely successful. "I just spoke to Larissa Cavender and Deputy Warren. Her place was broken into. She and her husband had driven to the waterfront in Everett for an early dinner. She'd taken some boxes of the nicer things she had into the house and stowed them in a closet in a guest bedroom. Good thing, because the garage was trashed. This guy hasn't developed any patience."

"That's awful!" Erin dropped into her usual chair at the table. "She's a nice lady, and she works hard at bringing in at least a part-time income from eBay sales."

"That was my impression, too." Those furrows carved on Sam's face deepened again. "I'm mostly glad her husband was around when this happened. Probably the guy wouldn't have waited for her to get home, but…"

Erin shuddered. Sam reached over the table to clasp her hand. She let herself hold on, wondering if he had any idea how grateful she was to have him here.

He sighed. "Is Toby asleep?"

Erin nodded. "I think I'll get started in the garage. I… feel like we're running out of time."

Eyes sharp, Sam didn't even try to dispel her uneasiness. "I want to tell you to take the rest of the evening off but—" He grimaced, then tried to turn it into a grin. "Lead on, Ms. Reed. You're the tour guide."

The awful face she made at him relaxed his smile into something more like the real thing.

He nodded his approval when she propped open the door leading into the garage. She set up a couple of folding card tables and chairs and, with a mental shrug, chose a tower of stacked plastic tote bags of varying vintage and colors for them to start with.

Sam only had to ask her opinion once, when he found a snarl of jewelry, scarves, high heels and what appeared to be a hopelessly snagged wedding veil.

She dug deeper with him hovering over her and came up with two shawls, a tattered feather boa and two cheap tiaras. No fingers, tongues or anything else unpleasant.

"Dress-up collection to pull out when kids need to be entertained or are determined to put on a show," she said.

"Seriously?"

She laughed at his expression. "Really. They're invaluable. In this case, I think that's all thrift store at best."

He put the lid back on and carried it to the designated thrift store pile.

She found a rock and mineral collection, which included some nice hunks of amethyst and other crystals as well as fossils she'd be able to sell. As heavy as it was, Erin had Sam drag it to a spot near the door. Valuing every specimen would be time-consuming, but worth it. Once she had time…

"I'll bet Toby would like some of those," Sam commented as he carried another tub to his card table.

"Of course he would," she mumbled. Now she'd feel guilty if she didn't choose some of the nicest pieces to go on a shelf in Toby's room.

At 9:30 p.m., she called a halt. She'd just finished digging through the contents of a tub and decided she needed better light to see whether some of the fabrics were salvageable when she realized it was her bedtime.

Sam looked surprised, then grinned crookedly. "Forgot about your alarm."

She wrinkled her nose. "I never dare to unless I want to sleepwalk through the next day."

Sam readily put back into place the lid he'd just peeled off, stood and turned his head, clearly evaluating the monumental task that lay ahead. He muttered something under his breath she didn't catch and didn't ask him to repeat.

"When I work out here, Toby likes to play hide-and-seek. He finds me right away, but *he* invariably finds new places to hide. Every time we move a few boxes or I pull furniture out and shift other things, voila! It's all new and different."

Amusement curved his mouth. "That might be fun."

A few minutes later, they turned out the lights and locked the garage door. *Moment of truth*, she thought.

"Um… I don't know what you want to do about sleeping, but, well, if you'd like to share my bed, that's okay."

"Was that an invitation?"

This time, she managed a simple, "Yes."

"Is Toby in his own room?"

"Yes, and he sleeps like a log. Besides, at his age he won't think a thing of it if he finds you in bed with me."

"Thank God." She hadn't known how still Sam had been, until he crossed the kitchen and gathered her into his arms with a speed that left her dazzled.

SAM AWAKENED FROM an astonishing dream when the woman in his dream—no, in bed with him—eased away. He reached for her, but she evaded his hands.

"I hear Toby," she murmured.

Toby. Oh, man. Now Sam *really* didn't want to wake up.

"You can sleep a little longer if you want…"

He rubbed a hand over his face and opened his eyes. "Only if you'll come back to bed."

"Uh-huh. Sure." She laughed as she backed away.

A minute later, she left the room with a pile of clothes in hand, and he heard her and Toby talking briefly, then the sound of the shower. Yeah, he could use one of those. A neat pile of his clean clothes she'd deposited on her dresser meant he didn't have to squeeze in a trip home to restock his wardrobe. He momentarily felt a pang of guilt for the horses, but he'd called a neighbor boy yesterday who had his own horse and had cared for Sam's before.

After breakfast, he started work again in the garage while Erin got Toby settled with a coloring project at the kitchen table. She hadn't appeared yet when his phone rang with a call from an unfamiliar number.

He answered, identifying himself, and a woman said, "My name is Marsha Van Beek. I own the antique and collectibles mall where Erin Reid has a space. She gave me your number in case of a problem."

"What happened?"

The answer to his question was predictable: a break-in and burglary had occurred sometime during the night. Ms. Reed's space was one that had suffered some of the most attention and damage.

He assured her he'd tell Erin.

Yes, Ms. Van Beek had installed a burglar alarm, but wires had been cut to disable it. It was an old one, and she'd been thinking about replacing it. No, she hadn't called 9-1-1 yet. He asked her to do so and promised to be there within twenty minutes.

He pocketed his phone just as Erin appeared in the doorway to the garage.

"Toby will be happy for half an hour or so." She stopped. "Something's wrong." Then she shook her head. "More wrong."

When he gave her the latest news, she listened in silence. Finally, she said, "Do you think it was that guy who was so weird?"

"I do, but Ms. Van Beek says she should have some camera footage."

"I'd forgotten she had cameras. Thank goodness! But what about the security system?"

"Bypassed. Sounds like it was an antique. Pun intended."

"I need to go with you. Only—"

Sam shook his head. "You won't want Toby to see the damage. And remember, Patrick should be here shortly."

She waffled briefly over whether she should take her son

to daycare, then said, "Yesterday was a long day for him. Maybe I can drop him off for a couple hours later today, just to see what needs to be done at the booth and how much I should plan to bring to fill gaps."

He stepped toward and held out his arms. "C'mere."

The way she melted into him, she needed the contact as much as he did. When at last she straightened away from him, he said, "I'll call when I know more. Don't open the door without being sure it's Patrick."

She promised. Sam stuck his head in the kitchen and admired Toby's artwork, kissed Erin lightly and let himself out.

When he parked in front of the antique mall, a marked sheriff's deputy car was already there. He rapped on the glass door, and a woman with improbably blue hair let him in.

"Detective McKeige?"

"Yes. You're Ms. Van Beek?"

"Marsha, please. There's a deputy here—"

"I saw. Show me what part of the business got hit." What he could see of the store near the entrance appeared fine; expansive windows and glass doors had offered some protection, since anyone inside—presumably using a flashlight—would have been too visible to any late passing traffic.

It was no surprise that Erin's double-space was at the center of the burglary and vandalism. He winced at the sight and spoke briefly to the deputy.

A dozen other spaces had also been hit. Some had been left alone; apparently the burglar hadn't been interested in antique tools, used vinyl records and books or textiles that seemed to include quilts, crocheted something—tablecloths? bedspreads?—and a basket filled to the brim with neatly pressed handkerchiefs. Did people still use those?

Focus.

Studying the carnage, he decided the burglar also hadn't been interested in furniture. Because it would be hard to re-sell? Or because he'd been alone, and hauling bigger pieces would have been beyond him?

This quarter of the mall was closest to the back entrance. The wires had been cut on a primitive security system on the back door.

He and Deputy Garvin joined to study the obvious gaps in merchandise—and the spiteful damage that had been the result of temper or done just for fun. China dishes were smashed, furniture thrown to the floor and in many cases broken, and shelving units pushed over. There were no marks of an ax. This looked, in fact, a lot like what he'd seen in the Snohomish antique dealer's garage and sev-eral other break-ins. That didn't mean the creep after Erin wasn't responsible, but Sam's gut said not now that he was at the scene.

The camera footage was lousy quality. He suspected those cameras were as old as the security system. Grainy or not, he was able to watch a man coming and going, car-rying as much as he could to the propped-open doors in back. The camera out there had caught an SUV, parked at a slant so that the license plate couldn't be seen.

The guy had used his head. He knew he was on film and didn't care, because he showed his finger to the cameras a couple of times. He wore a black hooded sweatshirt over jeans and work boots. His face was covered.

Sam ran the tape forward and back, leaning in close. He'd swear that was a bandanna versus the ski mask worn by the man who attacked Jeremy Conyers at the storage facility. Sam made note of how high up the cameras were installed and guessed the burglar to be medium height, nowhere near as tall as Sam himself was.

"I want Erin to watch this footage," he told the mall owner. "I imagine she told you about the odd duck who approached her one of the last times she was here."

"Yes, she did. But with his face covered, he'll be hard to recognize." Marsha shook her head. "But of course I'll make sure she watches this."

Erin was going to be mad as hell, Sam thought, and out a lot of money. He discussed insurance coverage with Marsha Van Beek and wondered if Erin carried individual coverage on the merchandise she displayed here. He hoped so.

The deputy agreed to call for a fingerprint tech. Marsha would keep the closed sign up for today at least and start calling the other individuals whose spaces had been affected. Sam went out to his truck to call Erin.

Once she confirmed that Patrick had arrived, Sam described what he'd seen as well as he could. She asked about a few individual items, but he had to keep saying, "I don't know. It's a mess." He admitted not seeing a glass-fronted, locked case. In fact, broken glass had littered the floor in her space, and he felt sure the pricier pieces she'd locked up were gone.

He wasn't surprised to learn that she did maintain a careful inventory of what she took to the mall and what had sold. She also noted when she removed something herself because it wasn't selling.

"I think I have to take Toby to Mrs. Hall's after lunch whether he likes it or not. We all need to clean up our spaces and restock so that Marsha can reopen without having to answer a million questions. Which means I won't be able to keep searching here." Erin paused to consider her next words. "Would it be out of line if I get Patrick to help me load my truck?"

Sam laughed. "No. We'll call it his lunch hour."

He made the snap decision to join her, help her clean up and haul in new stock. He worked a lot more than forty hours a week, and he was doing his job in part when he was with Erin.

Sleeping with her... Well, that wasn't any of his lieutenant's business. And he wasn't prepared to analyze how involved he'd become with Erin and her cute kid.

Chapter Fifteen

Erin knew what she'd see—Sam had sent her a couple of photos on his phone—but when she arrived at the mall, she was shocked nonetheless. Shouldn't she be inured by this time, given everything that had already happened?

Standing behind her, Sam wrapped his hands around her upper arms and gently squeezed. Somehow, that was all she needed.

"What a creep," she said.

"That's one way to put it."

She squared her shoulders. "Let me see the other spaces he hit."

Two of the tenants had beaten her here and were beginning to clean up. They hadn't lost as much as she had, but only because she had a double space.

From her position on her knees as she picked through a pile of shattered glass and porcelain, Linda Bradford glanced up. "This stinks!"

"It does, but we're not alone," Erin said. "I know a couple of eBay sellers who have had break-ins at home. Oh, and an antique dealer, too."

Linda, a usually good-natured, middle-aged woman, grimaced. "Misery loves company, huh?" She smiled wryly. "Yell if you need a hand."

Erin thanked her and returned to her own space. She'd brought a broom and dustpan plus some empty cardboard boxes and black plastic bags.

Sam asked her to watch the surveillance video before she started work. The murky black-and-white images surprised her, although she blew out an angry breath the first time the burglar flipped her off. She sat in silence as it ran, then Sam restarted it so she could watch again.

Finally, she shook her head. "I don't think it's that weird guy. This looks more like...not a teenager, but close."

"I had the same impression. Something about the way he moves."

"But how is he going to sell the stuff he took?"

"Online?"

Erin mulled over his suggestion. "There's a thought. Maybe I should start searching for a few of the more distinctive pieces of jewelry I lost. Oh, and that occupied Japan vase!"

"That's a good idea. He may not be dumb enough to list them right away, but you never know."

"If this isn't the same guy who broke into my place, then it's just chance he blew through my space here."

"I'm afraid so." Sam gave her a side-arm hug. "What can I do to help?"

"Oh..." Resisting the temptation to just lean on him, she looked around. "Let's rescue anything that isn't broken first, then sweep up. Marsha says we can put everything in the dumpster out back. She'll order a second one if we need it."

There wasn't an awful lot that proved to be salvageable. One bookcase with cabinet doors on the bottom had escaped damage despite being toppled over. Erin was mad about the glass-fronted case. She could have replaced the glass, but the wood had split down one side, too. Sam hauled it out back.

It was depressing how quickly they *did* clean up and to realize how much she'd lost. Marsha carried insurance that would cover some of the loss, once the tenants brought her lists of what had been stolen or broken and the value.

In the end, Erin looked around, made a mental list of what she should bring to start over again and gathered her cleaning supplies to go home for a first load.

SAM GAINED NEW respect for how hard she worked after assisting Erin that afternoon. Loading furniture into the back of her truck and his pickup, then unloading it and carrying it in at the other end was backbreaking word. Erin carried her half of the weight of each piece despite her fine-boned build. She had more muscle than showed.

This had to be done, so he didn't say a word about the sense of urgency riding him. He didn't remember ever having an investigation so tangled by what appeared to be unrelated crimes that just happened to *look* similar. Not only that, they were all occurring in a relatively rural, even peaceful part of the county.

If Erin hadn't found the box with the tongue and other less gruesome trophies, he might be speculating about whether the two sets of crimes were in fact related. As it was…he felt an itch every time he thought about the piles and piles of boxes and tubs filling Erin's two-car garage. There was more to be found, and this guy would be back soon.

He picked up burgers and fries for them all to eat for dinner, then got sucked into playing first a board game, then hide-and-seek out in the garage. Erin had been right—she was easy to find, but Toby, not so much. The kid could squirm into tiny spaces.

Every time, Sam couldn't help wondering if this tub or that one held more of a serial killer's goodies.

Given his dark thoughts, he almost decided to settle for cuddling Erin in bed that night, but seeing her slender, feminine body as she undressed changed his mind. Holding her after tender and then explosive lovemaking, he heard himself say, "It keeps getting better."

Her head bobbed where she rested it on his shoulder.

He didn't say, *I'm scared for you.* Or worse, *What if that scumbag got his hands on Toby, knowing you'd do anything to save your son?*

Sam hadn't ever gotten involved with a witness, victim or suspect in any investigation, and he didn't like the dread that hovered like a heavy raincloud whenever he wasn't with Erin *and* Toby. He was falling for both mother and child.

Strangely, the last thing he thought as he relaxed into sleep was, *I'm happy.*

Having so much at stake would only ratchet up his anxiety the next time he had to do his job and leave her to do hers.

Which happened a lot sooner than he expected.

AN ALARM OF some kind wrenched Sam out of a deep sleep. *What in...?* It took him longer than usual to surface enough to understand he was hearing his phone ringing.

While he groped for it, Erin mumbled as she struggled to untangle herself from the covers beside him.

His eyes found the digital numbers that read 4:17 a.m.

The number calling him looked familiar but wasn't identified.

He cleared his throat and answered. "McKeige."

"Detective." The male voice was pitched barely above being a whisper. "This is Jeremy. Conyers. You know."

"What's going on?"

"I bedded down tonight at my uncle's house. I've been working on it, you know."

Sam knew.

"I'm hearing sounds in the garage. What should I do?"

"Stay where you are. Hide, if whoever is in the garage tries to enter the house. Is that door locked?"

"I…don't remember. It's just a push button."

"Okay. I'm on my way, and I'm calling for a deputy to back me up. We'll approach without sirens or lights but blast them when we pull into your driveway. Do you understand?"

"Yeah." The voice was even shakier. "I think he must know I'm here."

If Conyers had parked in the driveway himself, he was right. The intruder was either stupid, reckless…or enjoyed knowing the terror he caused when he broke into an occupied home.

Sam was reaching for his pants before he even ended the call.

Erin sat up, clutching the bedclothes to her. "Who was that?"

"Conyers. He's at his uncle's. Somebody is in the garage. I've got to go."

Sounding shaken, she said, "Be careful."

Thank God he had a Kevlar vest in his vehicle.

Conyer's uncle's place was less than half a mile from

Erin's house. Idling a block away, Sam waited for backup. Unfortunately, the deputy radioed to let him know he'd been called to the scene of a shooting.

"Deputy Barker is a half hour out," the deputy told him, stress in his voice.

"Okay." This was the price they paid, policing a largely rural part of the state studded with small towns that in most cases contracted with the county for their law enforcement. "You take care."

"You, too."

Wishing he had full-body armor, Sam knew he had to go in. If a neighbor had called in the report of an intruder and Sam didn't know Jeremy Conyers was cowering in the house, he could have waited for backup. As it was, he didn't think twice. He accelerated toward the house mid-block, hitting lights and siren at the last second.

Then he slammed to a stop, blocking the driveway, and dove out to hunker behind the engine block, gun in his hands.

For an instant, nothing happened. Then a light appeared in a window a couple of houses away. Others came on. He gritted his teeth. Didn't people use their heads? Curiosity could kill someone compelled to step out on a porch—

A light above what was probably the neighbor's patio let him see the side door into Conyers's garage swing open. A dark shape appeared.

Sam yelled, "This is the police. Put down your weapon and lie on the ground with your arms outstretched!"

A bullet pinged off the fender of his SUV even before he heard the crack of a gunshot. Without hesitation, he returned fire.

Answering fire kept him pinned down. The moment it

stopped, he ran for the corner of the garage, flattening his back before he peered into the narrow space. A thud and a squeak told him the scumbag had just thrown himself over a fence. Normally he'd have assumed someone flee-ing would jump into that next-door neighbor's yard...but not when it had outdoor lighting.

Instead of going for the obvious, Sam sprinted through an open gate into Conyers's backyard. He was betting his quarry had gone over the fence at the back of the yard, but he was too far behind to catch him that way.

Seconds later, he threw himself behind the wheel of his county SUV, turned off the siren and lights and left off his headlights. He drove to the closest cross street, irritated to see that several neighbors had come out onto porches or front lawns to rubberneck.

The moment Sam eased around the corner, he switched on his headlights but caught no movement. He accelerated toward the next street, turned that corner and saw a flash of red brake lights as a big dark vehicle made a turn.

Now he hit his flashers and siren and accelerated in pur-suit. He swore out loud. If only there'd been two of them here, they could have had this guy.

By the time he reached that corner, the vehicle, still driving without lights, had gained close to a block on him. It turned again. Sam followed but was losing ground. He was too aware that a dog might bolt out in front of him or a neighbor try to wave him down. There were reasons high-speed pursuits weren't a good idea, and in a packed neighborhood like this, any speed more than thirty miles an hour qualified.

Ten minutes later, he'd lost the guy.

He went on the radio to issue a BOLO, for what good that

would do with only a couple of deputies working this part of the county and both possibly tied up with the shooting.

Jaw clenched, he turned off the flashers and siren and drove back to Conyers's house. When he rang, Jeremy came to the door, eyes wild, wearing jeans and a baggy Seattle Seahawks sweatshirt that might have been his uncle's.

"What happened?" He peered past Sam. "Did you get him?"

"Unfortunately not. He went over the back fence and was parked on that block. I caught a glimpse of the vehicle, but he was really booking, no headlights so he was hard to see, and I had to be more cautious." His jaw ached from frustration. "I'd like to get a look in the garage."

"Come in. I did what you said and stayed in the bedroom."

"That was smart," Sam assured him.

The interior of this standard-issue ranch-style house was similar to Erin's, but more dated. Jeremy was going to have some work to do before he put this place on the market or moved in, if that was his intention.

The first glimpse into the garage startled Sam. Old metal file cabinets lined three sides and, as time went on, had been blocked by mountains of white banker's boxes that must hold files as well. A surprising number sat neatly in front of the garage door.

Closer to the interior door, heaps of paperwork had been tossed from boxes that were flung away. A few of the metal file cabinets lay on their sides, their contents adding to the heaps.

What riveted Sam was the red plastic two-gallon gas can sitting in the middle of the garage. No matches, but the would-be arsonist probably had those in his pocket.

"Son of a—" Jeremy muttered. "He was going to burn the place down."

"If he couldn't find what he was looking for. I'm half surprised he didn't—" Sam cut himself off. No point in scaring Jeremy more than he already had been.

But Jeremy understood. "If you'd had your siren on as you approached, he'd have had time to start a fire."

"That's not what I expected," Sam said grimly, "but you're right." He rubbed a hand over his scratchy jaw. "I assume you haven't found anything?"

"Nothing remotely current. I don't understand why Uncle Charles kept paperwork from decades ago. I mean, even when someone who was up-to-date on payments moves out, you might want to keep the records for a couple years in case there's an issue, but after that?"

"It probably just got away from him."

"Yeah." Jeremy's fear succumbed to depression. "But I can't throw anything away without looking at it first."

"What's the most recent date you've seen?"

He gave an unhappy laugh. "2009. That was in boxes at the front over where I started."

"Then I doubt you'll find anything relevant to the attack at your office. If you need to keep working on it, I suggest you do it in daylight with the garage door open and you staying aware. Otherwise, if you're not in any hurry to clear out the garage and house, you can lock up and stay away for now." Sam paused. "If you can afford it, I'd recommend you put a security system into place, or my bet is you'll have a mysterious house fire."

Jeremy groaned. "Yeah. Real estate prices are high enough these days, I sure don't want to lose the house. I haven't checked to find out what my uncle had it insured for, either."

"You'd better do that right away," Sam advised. "I'm going to put the gas can in the back of my SUV and get it checked for fingerprints."

"I sure don't want to leave it sitting here!"

Sam put on gloves, lifted the red can from the bottom to preserve any potential prints on the handle and carried it out the side door to his SUV.

Jeremy decided to lock up and drive home to shower and have breakfast before he opened the office at the storage facility.

"I take it you quit whatever job you had before your uncle died?" Sam asked.

"I moved back here to help out when Uncle Charles's health went downhill. He was my only family, since my parents are gone, and he and Aunt Marie didn't have kids. I haven't decided whether to sell the storage business and this house or stay. Either way, there's a lot of work ahead of me."

"I can see that." Two neighbors were advancing down the sidewalk toward them. Sam raised his voice. "Please go home. Mr. Conyers had a break-in, but the intruder is long gone."

Jeremy ignored them. "I'll lock up."

"I'll wait until you're ready to go." Fortunately, the curiosity seekers had reluctantly turned around and were shuffling in bathrobes and slippers back toward their own homes.

Jeremy was back in barely a couple of minutes. He'd left a light on inside the house, which Sam understood even if it wouldn't deter a man who'd broken into the garage with the full knowledge that someone was asleep in the house.

That kind of boldness wasn't common, but they already knew this guy was fully prepared to commit violence directed at anyone who got in his way.

Sam suspected he might actively *want* to hurt or kill the homeowners who thwarted his need to find his lost treasures. The thought was enough to stir the hairs on the back of his neck. He needed to get back to Erin's.

SINCE THERE WAS no way she could go back to sleep, Erin got up, put on her fleece robe and checked on Toby before she put water on to boil. Sam wouldn't have left without locking behind himself, but she checked both the front door and the one into the garage. As expected, they were secure.

She decided on English breakfast tea instead of the usual herbal; Sam would undoubtedly be gone at least an hour, and Toby would bound out of bed, cheerful and energetic, any time after six. For now, she just sat, something she rarely did.

Relaxing was impossible, though, so she started making a mental list of what else she could put in her space at the mall with the least effort. Before she knew it, she'd drifted into worrying about Sam and what he'd found at Jeremy's uncle's house. It helped to know he'd called for backup, but that was no guarantee he wouldn't get shot or plunge into a fiery inferno to rescue Jeremy or… Oh, she could come up with plenty of possibilities.

Please keep him safe.

Her thoughts didn't wander far, because it had become instinctive to listen for any sound that didn't belong. Twice she heard cars passing out front. Neither even hesitated in front of her house. She kept an eye on her phone, which she'd set right in front of her on the table.

If there were any tubs she or Patrick or Sam hadn't gone through already here in the house, she'd have gone to work, if only to occupy her attention. But there was no way she was going into the garage by herself, leaving Toby alone in the house. She shivered at the idea of opening the door to the garage, knowing how easily someone could hide out there. Finally, she started scrolling through online news, reading a few articles that she'd probably forget the minute Sam called or came home.

Except this wasn't his home.

She had the unsettling feeling she'd just driven over a speed bump. She'd let herself feel too much for a man she'd known all along was here because his job demanded he both keep her safe and find anything in her house that would help him nail the black-masked killer who'd left Jeremy to die in that rage-fueled fire. The same man who'd searched her garage and tried to open the door into the house when she and Toby were alone here.

Not inviting Sam into her bed would have been smart, she thought, feeling cold despite the heat coming through the vents and her thick fuzzy robe. But it was too late to close that door, and she didn't want to, anyway. She told herself it was okay to let herself enjoy the connection between him and Toby, savor his touch and his smile and the passion in bed that was so new to her. As long as she gave herself a bitter-tasting dose of reality often enough that she didn't succumb entirely to fantasy.

She glanced at the stove. He'd been gone for more than an hour now. Didn't he know she'd be worried? If he'd just text...

At the sound of the key in the lock, Erin shot to her feet.

That had to be him. Still, she hovered in the kitchen in case it *wasn't* him. She'd run to Toby's room and—

"Erin?" Sam said quietly, his eyes meeting hers before he closed and locked the door again.

She rushed to him, glad when his arms closed around her. The chillier air outside had come in with him. She hugged him and mumbled, "I was scared."

"Nothing to be scared about."

But something about his tone had her tilting her head back to see his face.

"You didn't catch him."

"No," he said shortly. His arms tightened. "My backup got diverted to another incident. I scared the guy out, we exchanged a few potshots, and he ran. He rocketed out of the neighborhood at speeds I couldn't match without risking an accident."

Her brain had stopped on the word *potshots*. "Wait. He *shot* at you?"

"Yeah. I have a couple of dents in my vehicle, and I think a bullet punched a hole in a window." His voice had lowered to a growl. "I'll have to report discharging my own firearm and go back in daylight to see if there are any traces of blood that would suggest I so much as winged him."

"So he's been carrying a gun." That hadn't occurred to her, although it should have.

Sam grunted. "That, or he picked one up recently."

"You could have been hurt." She wanted to feel numb but couldn't.

"Not likely. I have on a vest—"

That was why his already solid chest felt thicker.

"And most people aren't good shots. This guy is consumed by impulse and temper. I seriously doubt he's put in any time at a range."

"But all he had to do was point his gun in the right direction."

"At close range, that works. We were separated by twenty-five feet or more."

She'd believed Sam was invincible. Now she had to come to terms with the knowledge that she was in love with a man whose risk of being killed on the job had to be a lot higher than normal.

But surely violent crime wasn't common in eastern Snohomish County, she tried to persuade herself.

Someone had shot at him tonight.

She clenched her teeth to keep them from chattering and hugged him harder.

Chapter Sixteen

Sam wanted to hustle Erin back into her bedroom, strip off the robe and make love to her. The moment he set eyes on her, that was all he could think about. Unfortunately, a desperate glance at the clock told him it wasn't happening. Toby would be bouncing into the kitchen anytime.

Sam hoped she hadn't noticed his erection before she backed off, chattering about pouring him a cup of coffee and how she ought to get dressed.

He grimaced. She'd noticed, all right, or her cheeks wouldn't be pink. This was a drawback to getting involved with a woman who had a child.

How far he'd come, he thought in bemusement; two weeks ago, he wouldn't have considered doing any such thing, and not because a kid was an inconvenience. When was the last time he'd thought of Michael when he was with Toby? He couldn't call up the last instance. The boys were no more alike than Erin was like Ashley, thank God.

He hoped Erin was thinking the same way. It wasn't a good time to raise the subject, though. In fact, his priority had to be keeping mother and son safe.

No, he hadn't forgotten what mattered most.

Toby appeared soon enough, followed by the arrival of

the young deputy who had dived into what he might have considered a tedious job with seemingly genuine dedication.

Knapstad glanced at Sam. "Looks like your vehicle took some damage," he said in a low voice.

Sam grunted. "Unfortunately, that means I'll have to leave you two—three—on your own again while I get it looked at and fill out some reports." He briefly summed up the early-morning events and heard in return about the shooting, which had been a drive-by that left two victims hospitalized. Since witnesses saw the incident and one of them had had the rare presence of mind to memorize the license plate in question, two stoned guys in their early twenties were now behind bars.

Once they were up-to-date on news, Sam told Erin about his intentions, and she promised to stick close to home this morning. "I do have to take more stuff to the mall and mail some packages I have ready to go for eBay, but I can do that later in the afternoon."

He didn't want her near the mall but understood she needed to keep making a living. "If I'm back in time, I'll help you load and maybe go with you."

She opened her mouth, probably to argue that she usually did it on her own, but then closed it and clamped her lips together. She had to share his nervousness about the mall even though she agreed that the break-in and damage probably were separate from the obsession and violence that accompanied the killer who was sure to be back to her house.

"Keep your gun close," he ordered Knapstad before leaving.

He hadn't made it out to the highway before his phone rang. Deputy Knapstad.

Sam answered at once, identifying himself.

"I found something." The young deputy's voice shook. "It's—uh, a hand. Mostly down to bone, but there's still polish on fingernails. It's, um, wearing a ring, too."

"I'm on my way back," Sam said, even as he gave a short burst of his siren, signaled and swung across the road to make a U-turn without slowing any more than he had to.

His heartbeat picked up. What else might be in the same container? How many more victims could they identify? Would they find something they could use to nail the killer?

ERIN MADE SURE Toby was occupied in his bedroom before she and Patrick hung over Sam as he donned latex gloves and picked through the contents of the tub that weren't materially different than those in the earlier one.

This was a killer who liked to collect the obviously feminine items worn by his victims. Oh, and their body parts, too.

In fact, a cardboard shoebox at the bottom revealed what had to be an ear complete with dangly sterling silver earring. The earring was tarnished, and the interior of the box splattered with rusty stains that turned her stomach. All their stomachs, maybe, since Patrick flinched and looked away, and Sam gently fit the lid back on the box.

She was surprised when he rotated the box to look at the end, until her gaze followed his. The box had held men's athletic shoes, size eleven and a half. The brand, model of shoe and store name were all emblazoned on the box.

Sam mumbled a few words he usually held back around her, then said, "Good work, both of you. I'll take this and start at the medical examiner's office."

She turned her head to look at the mountains of containers they had yet to search without any enthusiasm at all.

Usually going through unseen items she'd won in storage unit auctions was like treasure hunting. Aside from the amazing contents of the one storage unit, mostly what she found was mundane—at best worth twenty or thirty dollars. But there was always the thread of excitement because a box might have stoneware hand-painted with animals that looked primitive but was highly collectible or Navajo squash-blossom jewelry or a nineteenth-century weathervane. People didn't always know what they had. She remembered fondly the campaign buttons for Harry Truman she'd sold for a significant amount, for example.

A queasy feeling in her stomach, she knew that excitement might always be tempered by the possibility that *this* plastic tub could contain something gruesome.

She walked Sam into the house and to the door just because she wanted to, but his grim expression and the knotted muscles in his jaw told her he felt much as she did, even if he also hoped for leads from the latest find.

She and Patrick worked steadily after Sam left, and she took the occasional break to entertain Toby. Sandwiches and cookies filled their stomachs at lunch. Her ear stayed tuned for her phone to ring, but Sam wasn't likely to learn anything until he had fingerprint matches and, eventually, a DNA match.

He did call midafternoon to let her know that he'd had to take the county-owned SUV in for body work, after which he'd catch a ride back to sheriff's headquarters and check out a replacement vehicle.

Sounding weary, he said, "I do have a name to go with the ear. When I saw it, something niggled at me. When I searched for female murder victims that had been dismembered in any way, I noted a woman who'd had an ear cut off. The earring matches what she was wearing."

"Who was she?" Erin felt compelled to know.

"Her name was Renee Legare. Twenty-four-year-old, newly-minted real estate agent in Coeur d'Alene, Idaho."

"I've been there. It's beautiful." Picturing the magnificent lake and expensive homes surrounding it now felt obscene.

"Yeah. We keep expanding his territory."

Sam didn't have to identify who *he* was.

"I don't think I'll make it back until close to five," he added. "Can you hold off the antique mall run until morning?"

"You can't follow me around everywhere I go. Don't you already have more threads you need to follow?"

"I'm waiting for a call back from the detective who investigated Ms. Legare's death," he admitted.

"I'll be careful. It should be a busy day at the mall. Usually I can get someone else to help me bring everything in."

"And walk you out," he said sternly.

"And walk me out." She didn't really have her fingers crossed behind her back, but she was envisioning them as if she did.

Patrick did his best to help her load, but given his walking cast, she felt guilty letting him lift anything. During the short drive, it was a struggle to smile and respond to Toby's chatter. The sickening knowledge of the latest finds hung over her, along with the fact that Sam's afternoon was partly busy with replacing his police vehicle because the one he'd been using was now *pocked by bullets*. Some must have come a lot closer to striking him than he'd admitted.

Surely this will be over soon, she thought. Or was it half prayer? Once forensic evidence produced a name, they'd also have photos, if only the dismal ones from driver's licenses, and then they could *look* for him. He was staying somewhere, buying groceries. People would have seen him. That he was faceless was possibly the creepiest part of all this.

After parking in back of the antique mall, she got lucky when two men who had a space exited together. They spotted her and walked over to offer to help her get everything in. She thanked them, grateful to have some extra time to arrange and rearrange her stock to be as appealing as possible.

When Toby got bored, she produced a handheld electronic game from her purse. He pounced on it, since she limited his time with it. The beeps seemed pitched to be annoying, if only to an adult ear.

She'd been right that this would be a busy day, which meant she chatted with browsers and took the name and number for a guy looking for a treadmill that she had in her garage. She kept meaning to list it on Craigslist, since it didn't quite fit here, and it wasn't the kind of thing you popped in the mail. Think how much space selling it would open up!

She took Marsha her list of stolen and damaged items and estimated value and was glad to hear that sales had risen steadily this year. One tenant who had suffered the most loss from the break-in had decided to give up her space. Marsha had a list of people who wanted in, but she offered it to Erin first.

The idea was tempting, but Erin didn't want to overextend herself. She worried about shortchanging Toby as it was. Since Jeremy Conyers hadn't come up with any information on the previous owners of the valuable contents of the storage unit, she ought to start work on photographing, describing and valuing everything.

And, of course, the days she'd spent searching everything she had piled up at home in search of a serial killer's precious collection had put her way behind.

Patrick called to let her know he hadn't found anything else and was heading home. He assured her he'd locked up.

It was almost five, and Toby, who hadn't had a nap, was drooping. That set her to trying to think of a dinner she could produce quickly. She also wished that Sam would be there waiting for them.

THE FINGERPRINTS FROM this latest tub opened up half a dozen new avenues for Sam to explore. The prints on the plastic lid especially matched those on the other one, not surprisingly. Ditto those on some of the items inside, including the shoebox and a couple of items that best held prints. What might be as many as four victims were identified. Sam sat down to make calls.

Time got away from him once he connected with the first investigator, then received return calls from two others. They reacted much as the ones he'd spoken to after the first discoveries. Anger and determination infused their voices, but again the names of men they'd looked closely at didn't match those at other crimes scenes.

The third detective said, "This wasn't my case, you understand. The original investigator retired with the understanding I would try not to let this go cold. You know, we all have ones that get to us. I'm wondering if he had some thoughts that didn't make it into the record. If I can get in touch with him, do you mind if he calls you?"

"No, I'd be glad to mine him for whatever he knows."
Every investigator considered possibilities they weren't able
to pursue for one reason or another or crossed off because
they seemed unlikely or reached a dead end.

At five o'clock, Sam left the desk he'd borrowed, took a
last look to be sure he wasn't forgetting anything...and of
course that was when his phone rang.

Rolling his shoulders to release some of the tension, he
answered, "Detective McKeige."

A gruff voice said, "My name is Frank Billman. I'm the
retired detective I hear you want to talk to."

"I do, indeed." Sam sat back down. He could talk on the
drive back to Erin's house, but then his attention would be
split between the conversation and traffic. This might not
take long.

"This about Julia Keele?"

"Yes." Sam explained about Erin and the storage business, leading up to what had to be trophies collected by a
killer—including from Ms. Keele. "I gather no body parts
were taken from her—"

Billman made a sound of horror.

Sam hurried on, "But we found her fingerprint on a pen-
dant in the latest box. As you know, I spoke to Detective
Shanks, and he thought you might recall something that
you hadn't included in your notes."

"Don't know for sure what I did note," the older man
said slowly. "No, I thought I'd ruled out one fellow, so I
might not have mentioned him."

"Him?"

"Name was... Let me think. Sawyer, I remember that
because it's not a common first name. Sawyer Wilkins!"
Billman sounded triumphant. "That's it. The guy made me

real uneasy, but I didn't have enough cause to fingerprint him or even bring him in for an interview. I regretted for a while that I hadn't collected a fingerprint surreptitiously, but I knew the DA wouldn't act on it."

"There's still a lot of reluctance," Sam agreed.

"I guess Ms. Keele had taken a couple to look at a house—she was a real estate agent—and this fellow hovered out front. When she and the couple came back out, he asked if she could show *him* the house. She suggested he make an appointment with her for another time, since she was committed to showing the couple several more places. He took her card, that's what she told a friend, but hoped he didn't call."

"So he made her uneasy, too."

"Sounds like it. He'd given her his name, and I tracked him down, but Ms. Keele hadn't disappeared until a couple of days after that encounter. He said he went ahead and had another agent show him some houses instead of waiting."

"You confirmed he did."

"Yep. Like I say, I didn't have enough excuse to look hard at him."

"But you wanted an excuse."

"I did. Just a gut feeling."

Sam got those, too. "Nobody of that name came up in any of the investigations into the attacks and/or murders of other victims, but that doesn't mean anything. No one name came up twice with all the investigations put together."

"The friend who told me about this guy said Ms. Keele would have been willing to show him houses if he'd had a wife, but he seemed intense, and she didn't want to be alone with him."

Plenty of murderers came across as normal to their coworkers or neighbors. It was less common for people to say he gave them the creeps. But Sam couldn't help thinking about the man who'd waylaid Erin at the antique mall, his behavior distinctly *off* even before he'd grabbed her.

"I'll track down this Sawyer Wilkins," Sam said. "Thank you for calling. If you think of anything else…"

"I'll get on the horn," the retired detective assured him. "If something comes of this—"

"I'll let you know. I promise."

Sam hesitated after ending the call. He was already going to be later than he'd told Erin to expect him, but man, he wanted to do a search. It shouldn't take long, so he opened his laptop again and typed in the name. It popped up, and he prowled through multiple databases, scrutinizing the couple of images he found. Typical DMV, they weren't good, but he was willing to bet they were good enough for Erin to recognize if Wilkins had been the man at the mall. He printed them.

And then he straightened, as if electrified by what he saw on the screen. A Sawyer Wilkins had been a person of interest in a rape case in Spokane, Washington, not far from the Idaho border. Almost had to be the same guy, except… Sam frowned. If they'd taken him seriously, his fingerprints should be in the system. So maybe this was another dead end.

He couldn't leave it at that, though. Swearing, he dialed the number for the detective squad in Spokane. Probably too late in the day to get anyone, but even the distant possibility he'd found his perpetrator didn't let him put this call off until morning.

He was placed on hold, and while he waited, he checked with Deputy Knapstad. The rookie said he had let Erin know he was leaving her house locked up behind him. "She sounded fine, but she was running later than she expected."

Good. With luck, Erin wouldn't be too far ahead of him at her house.

A voice abruptly replaced elevator music. "This is Detective Throndsen. What can I do for you?"

Sam had the spiel down pat now.

Throndsen grunted. "Not my investigation, but let me take a look."

Sam waited, not so patiently, until the other man came back on.

"The detective who had that case thought he'd found his man. The victim didn't see a face—I guess he wore a mask of some kind—but we have fingerprints." He went quiet again for a couple of minutes. "The detective died suddenly from an aneurysm. His more active cases eventually got picked up by someone else, but this Wilkins had evidently done a bunk, so that one has gone cold."

"Were the fingerprints entered?"

Throndsen didn't sound happy—what investigator would have?—when he admitted, "It doesn't look like it. Can I follow up on this?"

"I'd appreciate it. I hope they haven't disappeared at the lab."

"Me, too." He took the info from Sam and ended the call as abruptly as he started it.

Sam was sometimes wrong when he felt this tingle between his shoulder blades, but not often.

ERIN COULDN'T REMEMBER the last name of the man who sold old tools in the booth near her—he didn't sell at a volume that required him to update his inventory anywhere near as often as she did—but nobody else seemed to be in the vicinity. In fact, the whole place was looking deserted, even though it stayed open until six.

She glanced at her phone to realize it was a lot later than she'd thought it was. Maybe she'd secretly hoped Sam would show up to walk her out to her car himself.

When she told James Whatever-his-name-was that she'd been having some trouble and asked if he'd walk her and Toby out, he agreed readily. "I heard about the mess here a couple of days ago. I don't blame you for being nervous."

She opened her mouth to explain that her problems went beyond the break-in, then closed it. Really, this wouldn't take him five minutes, so she just smiled and thanked him. Toby was tired enough that she swung him up to her hip, and James of the rusty tools fell in behind her as they headed to the back of the building. Did she dare let Toby nap this late in the day?

As she reached for the door handle, she heard a strange sound behind her, a gasp, and then a thud. Erin had started to turn in alarm when a man's hands wrenched Toby from her hold.

"What are you—"

Oh God, oh God. He wore a black-knit face covering and had clamped a hand over Toby's mouth. Her little boy was waking up, beginning to struggle, but outmuscled.

"If you do anything to draw attention, you'll never see your kid again," the man who had control of her child snarled. "Do you hear me?"

The scream stayed trapped in her throat, and she bobbed her head.

"Give me your purse."

She'd already stuck her hand in to grab her phone but pulled it out and did as he'd asked.

He jerked his head to the door that she'd let close again. "Out."

What could she do but obey, even as she prayed there'd be other people here in back?

Except, now that she knew this killer was undoubtedly armed, would that be a good thing?

Chapter Seventeen

Once she had the heavy door open, he planted a hand on her back and shoved so hard she staggered. As she righted herself, she scanned the gravel parking lot, but only four vehicles were left. The one closest to the door was Marsha's.

"Straight ahead."

Out of the corner of her eye, she saw her own pickup truck, but of course he wouldn't want to take that. He had to be able to make a getaway after—

She couldn't let herself go there.

The big black SUV was right on the other side of her pickup, where it wouldn't catch the eye of anyone passing on the street.

It beeped as they approached. He opened the back door.

"Kid!" he snapped. "Lie down on the floor. You hear me? Your mom will be up with me. I'll hurt her if you try anything."

Toby whimpered. The last glimpse Erin had of his face showed it wet with tears as he was tossed forward, catching himself to curl up onto the floorboards. A hard hand on Erin's arm wrenched her forward.

"Quit whining! You help me find my stuff, and you might survive."

She knew the voice. This was the creepy man who'd

asked such weird questions that day. Which meant he was also a serial killer—and sick enough to cut off a victim's tongue, another one's ear and yet another woman's *hand*. And who knew what else they'd find in other tubs, if they had the chance to look?

If she'd thought she could throw herself out fast enough to also open the back door and grab Toby, she'd have done it. Instead, she sat. Her purse… He must have tossed it on the back seat, out of her reach. After a moment, she clicked the seat belt across herself.

"Mommy!" Toby cried.

"Shh," she said. She might have lied to reassure him, but their captor had climbed in behind the wheel and fired up the engine. He'd also pulled a handgun from somewhere and let it lie on his lap where she couldn't miss seeing it.

She'd never wanted a gun of her own, never fired one in her life, but right this minute, she knew she could and would shoot someone this close. Except, if she'd carried a gun, it would have been in her purse, as out of reach as her phone.

Gravel crunched under the tires as this brute drove forward and put on a signal before making the turn onto the road. In one of the holes in the mask, she could see his teeth, his lips drawn back from them.

I'm shaking, she realized and made herself stare straight ahead. *Sam will come.* Did this man know a cop had the key to her house and had been spending nights?

The drive was both too quick and felt as if it took forever.

Erin was careful not to turn her head as they approached her house, but her eyes darted down the side street and the block beyond her driveway. Sam still parked a distance away, so it wouldn't be obvious he was here.

Maybe it would be better if he *wasn't*. What if he came to

greet them and met a bullet instead? He wouldn't be wearing a Kevlar vest when he was anticipating dinner instead of a confrontation. If he arrived later instead, he'd instantly know they shouldn't be in the garage. He might even hear a voice that shouldn't be here.

Her captor didn't park in the driveway, either, but he did pull to the curb less than half a block away. The better to load his treasures once she led him to them, Erin thought semi-hysterically. If only she had the slightest idea of the location of more of his boxes.

He turned off the engine, said, "Stay," and jumped out, coming around too quickly. He opened the back door first and lifted Toby out, then came to her door. Of course, he'd grabbed her purse, too. "Walk beside me." His voice was guttural. "If you see anyone you know, wave."

Her teeth chattered at a volume she hoped he didn't hear. She didn't know whether to be glad none of her near neighbors were out and about or not.

She tried to project comfort to Toby, but it was hard when his mouth was round with a silent wail and snot and tears both smeared his face.

The man stopped on the welcome mat. "Keys?"

"In my pocket." She'd gotten them out earlier so she didn't have to set down Toby to hunt for them.

He held out his hand for them, quickly picked out the house key and pushed open the door. He tossed the keys inside and pulled his gun, listening for a minute before easing inside, ready to fire.

Silence met them. No Sam.

Erin bit her lip until she tasted blood as she followed him inside.

He closed and locked the door, looked around and shook his head. "No wonder you can't find anything."

Oh, she wanted to protest the contempt in his voice but clamped her mouth shut. Should she tell him they had, in fact, found two tubs with his obscene collectibles in them?

No. As volatile as he'd seemed at her booth the first time, she thought he'd be so enraged she and Toby wouldn't survive until Sam got home.

"You must know how to find what I want." His eyes glittered at her through the holes in the mask.

"No. How can I? I don't even know if I *have* whatever it is you're looking for!"

His hand slid around Toby's throat.

She closed her eyes. "I...assume it's not furniture."

"No. Plastic tubs, like these." He nodded toward the piles that still filled too much of the living room.

"If you can tell me what's in them...or what color they are?"

He shrugged. "They're older ones. Blue or green, maybe? Not like these." He kicked a particularly sturdy, newer style in black accented by bright yellow.

"Um...how many did you have?"

"Four."

"I never would have bid on the contents of a storage unit that had so little in it."

"I had a key to—" the hesitation was almost infinitesimal, but she heard it "—a relative's unit." His anger had ratcheted. "Didn't know he was dead for long enough, that damned place sold everything!"

"Okay." She tried to keep her tone soothing. His hand had loosened from around Toby's throat. "I've looked through every tub inside the house. That pile—" she pointed "—is going to a thrift store. Those—" she signaled with her head "—have things I need to list online or will put in my space at the antique mall."

His eyes narrowed at her. "You've been looking for my things."

"Um, well, kind of, because the police told me you'd gone to the houses of some of the other people that bid on stuff in storage units. And....I assume that was you in my garage that night." She dampened her lips. "I could tell you if I'd found anything that might be yours if I knew what was in your boxes."

What she could see of his grin was so savage, she recoiled at the sight.

"You'd know if you'd found it."

Please, Sam.

"Oh, okay." She hated the tremor in her voice. "Well, then if I have anything of yours, it has to be in the garage."

His eyes narrowed to slits as he stared at her. "You'd better not be lying to me."

"I'm not." That came out steadier.

He dropped her purse and kicked it between piles, then strode to the door to the garage. His hand had left Toby's throat, but he gripped him hard, and weirdly, as if he was a strangely shaped parcel, not a small human being. He wouldn't feel a qualm about murdering a three-year-old.

If there was some way to remove Toby from the equation. *Please, God, let Toby stay quiet.*

She'd swear she heard the faint ring of her phone as the heavy steel door swung closed behind them.

"Where are they?" he demanded.

"I don't know. And that's the truth," she said hastily, when she saw his shoulders start to bunch in rage. "I...

don't keep any kind of order. It doesn't matter to me which things came from what unit or garage sale or when I bought it." She bit her lip. "Although, it may help if you could tell me how long ago the unit your things were in might have been sold."

His lips curled back from his teeth. "Stolen from me, you mean."

"I… I can see why you'd see it that way."

"It might have been six or eight months ago."

Oh, boy. No wonder those tubs were scattered. It was a miracle they'd found any of them.

"Let's…just look for plastic tubs that *could* be yours. Oh, they wouldn't be over there. I just went through those." And found one of his, which suggested the remaining two might not be deeply buried.

When he glanced down at Toby, her heart constricted. The intruder had dropped him atop a couple of tubs. Toby's eyes met hers, and she shook her head silently.

"What about over here?" she said. After a moment of hesitation, he complied more than she anticipated, following her what might have been ten feet.

This might be as good as it got. She drew in a deep breath and yelled, "Hide, Toby! Go hide and seek!"

Her son uncurled.

The man started to lunge back toward him. Erin threw herself at him and hung from his arm. He tripped, they tangled…and Toby rocketed from his perch and vanished into the maze.

WHY WASN'T SHE answering?

Don't get paranoid, Sam told himself. She might be in

the bathroom helping Toby wash his hands or had just left her phone in her purse and didn't hear the ring.

But he didn't like it. Two minutes later, he tried again. The third time she didn't answer, he hit his lights and sirens and sped down Highway 2 toward Monroe and beyond.

If she picked up the phone, she'd have to see the string of notifications and would call him. Would she really be so careless with her phone, given what was going on?

He didn't believe it.

Calculating to keep himself from panic, he tried to decide whether to enter by the front door or the new side door into the garage, to which he'd kept a key when he installed it. If she was there—if *he* was there with her—they'd be in the garage.

If this monster killed Toby or Erin, Sam didn't know if he had a damn thing left to live for.

He shook the thought off. He wouldn't believe he'd be too late. He couldn't function if he let himself grieve prematurely. Normally his goal would be to arrest a serial killer so he could be convicted in multiple jurisdictions and give closure to his many victims' families. Vivid images of killing that piece of scum himself raced through his head instead.

He could circle the house first. Crash through a window if he saw them.

No, it had to be the garage.

"You bitch!"

The man slugged her so hard, her head snapped back. Darkness crept over her vision. *Toby.* She couldn't black out. She couldn't. But she did crash to the floor, and the back of her head bounced off the concrete.

Erin had to curl onto her side and breathe through the hammer blows of pain and the nausea that followed.

"Get up! If you don't get that kid back here, I'll shoot him when I do find him. You hear me?"

She tried to get to her hands and knees. "You don't need him. I know I can't fight back."

He kicked her hard enough to throw her back several feet. He'd connected with her hip, adding a stabbing pain. "Get up!"

She tried again. He grabbed her upper arm this time and yanked her to her feet.

"Find my boxes."

"Been trying," she mumbled.

"Do better."

"You should recognize them." She'd wanted to snap but it came out as another mumble.

The rage in his eyes would have terrified her if she hadn't somehow moved past that. *Endure.* Sam would come. She had to be alive for Sam. Even if he didn't love her, she knew what it would do to him if, after the crushing loss he'd suffered, he found her and Toby dead.

She swayed but took a step toward the piles of boxes she'd tried to direct this monster toward before. This time, he looked. When he didn't like the first tubs at the top, he threw them to one side so he could peel off the top of whatever one appeared familiar. Lids and contents flew. The crash of breaking glass and porcelain meant nothing right now.

His fingers bit hard into her arm as he dragged her on.

She wished she'd better seen which way Toby had gone. *Hide-and-seek.*

AFTER NOTING ERIN'S empty driveway, Sam locked onto the large black SUV immediately. He entered the license plate number in notes on his phone. No time to run it. He parked just out of sight around the corner, leaped out and closed the door with care so the sound wouldn't carry.

Vest… He didn't want to take time for that, either, but made himself. It might give him the chance to win a gunfight rather than go down immediately.

He'd already decided on the front door. He donned the Kevlar vest with awkward shrugs and dealt with the fastenings one-handed as he jogged the short distance, crossed the lawn and ascended the two porch steps. This was one occasion he'd have been glad of darkness, but daylight in the Northwest in early September still left long days.

Keys out. It only took him a fumbling second to find the right one… Insert it as carefully as if he were doing brain surgery… Turn it until he felt the click more than heard it… Gently turn the knob. The door opened. He hesitated, pushed it wide and entered with his weapon held in front of him.

The house was quiet. *Nobody here*, the quiet said. He eased in, placing his feet with care. Clear the kitchen and bedrooms first? His gut said no. Unless he was deluded, they had to be in the garage.

He laid his hand on the doorknob and turned it. It wasn't locked, and he didn't believe the young deputy would have left the house *without* locking even this interior door.

Sam eased it, too, open to the smallest of cracks. And that was when he heard an ugly string of obscenities followed by a thud and the sound of something shattering and knew he'd been right.

THE MASKED MAN was losing it, as wild as he'd been when she first set eyes on him in the storage facility office. Some distant part of Erin's brain wondered how he ever stalked his victims when he entirely lacked patience.

They worked their way along a serpentine gap between the next stacks. This wasn't one of Toby's favorite hiding places. By chance, half or more of the plastic tubs here were high quality, newer ones, which enraged the serial killer.

"But there are older ones here—"

"You're wasting my time!" He grabbed her and flung her into a pile of the boxes, which teetered. One at the top dropped down the other side.

Now her shoulder joined the chorus of pain. "We have to look here," she said again.

With no place to throw boxes in his way, he was driven to restacking them, the set of his face and the dark glitter in his eyes awakening fear that had almost vanished in numbness.

They reached the end. Erin hurried ahead back toward the gorgeous furniture. *Get him past*, she told herself. If he threw a fit here—

He didn't even look at the furniture or the musical instruments in cases or the spectacular lamp that she had wanted to be a genuine Tiffany but probably wasn't.

They had reached the slightly more open space close to the garage door when the metal door into the house swung wide.

"Down on the floor!" Sam yelled.

The man crouched behind the barricade of boxes, locked his fingers around her ankle and pulled his gun from what had to be his waistband.

She couldn't move until he suddenly released her, stood and fired. *Pop, pop, pop.*

Frantic that Sam had been hit, she saw that he'd retreated behind the metal door. But now he emerged, coolly firing his own weapon.

She seized the chance to scuttle a few feet away and crouched. More bullets flew. That metal door would never look the same again.

Erin hunkered low, only feet from that gorgeous lamp. She remembered how heavy it was: solid bronze and the thick glass of an earlier era.

"Back off, or I'll kill her!"

She knew he wouldn't hesitate to do that, but he hadn't turned the gun her way, not yet.

When Sam emerged again, a sliver of him mostly shielded by the door, she lunged for the lamp, lifted it and swung as if she was still a star batter on her high school softball team. *He* was turning, that hateful man who'd hurt her, as she moved. He got off at least one shot. She was so focused on her swing, she didn't think of her peril.

The shade of the lamp smashed into his head, as if it were a jack-o-'lantern that could be pulverized. The sound was awful despite the thin knit mask. Seeing him collapse as if his strings had been cut, she dropped the lamp, turned her back and fell to her knees. Her stomach revolted, and she started to dry heave.

At first she couldn't make out what Sam was yelling, but finally heard, "Erin! Is he down?"

She lifted one hand and waved.

The next moment, Sam was on his knees beside her. He took in the sight of the bloody mess a few feet away, then used his foot to nudge the handgun that had fallen to the concrete floor and edged it well away from the fallen man. In case he came back from the dead and groped for it, she thought blearily. Sam lifted the mask enough to seek a pulse. She could tell he didn't find one.

Then he came back to her, wrapped his arm around her and, rough and tender at the same time, said, "Come on, sweetheart. Let's step away. Can you stand?"

Her head bobbed.

"Where's Toby?"

"Hide-and-seek," she whispered.

"Okay." He supported her as she stood, then steered her toward the chairs around the card table.

Sinking into one, she asked, "Is he dead? Are you sure?"

"Pretty sure." He cleared his throat. "I'd be congratulating myself for getting here in time, but it appears you didn't need me."

"I did." Unable to dissemble, she felt tears pool in her eyes and start to fall as she looked up at him. "I do."

"God." His face contorted. "I was so afraid."

"Me, too."

He cupped her face, using his thumbs to wash away tears. "I don't ever want to lose you."

Now she cried in earnest.

He laughed, groaned and straightened. "Let me go rescue Toby."

At least the dead man's face and head were covered, but… "Don't let him see…"

"Wouldn't think of it." Sam walked past the shattered lamp and the body, then raised his voice. "Olly olly oxen free! Come on out, Toby."

After a too-long moment of complete silence, which had

Erin swiveling on the folding metal chair, a small voice sounded. "Sam?"

"Yup."

A minute later, Sam scooped up her small son and used his own big body to prevent Toby from seeing the fallen man.

The body. Because *she'd* killed him. Her stomach lurched again.

Somehow Sam convinced Erin to take Toby inside without him. By the time she reached the kitchen, she remembered how many places she hurt. But...no blood, as far as she could see. And Toby was intact, his body solid and wiry, his grip strong, his face blotchy from tears that no longer fell. He was fine.

She wanted to cry again but refused to allow herself. That would just scare him. Instead, she plopped him down on the raised seat on his chair at the table and said, "Thank goodness Sam got here, huh?"

"*Uh*-huh!" he agreed.

She heard the door open and close, and there was Sam walking toward them, his gaze never leaving hers. He must have made a call, since his phone was in his hand, and she envisioned what was to come: a dozen cops, flashing lights, an ambulance or two and EMTs who would peer at her and insist she go to the hospital for an MRI. There'd undoubtedly be questions, since she *had* killed a man, but she couldn't imagine anyone would really have trouble with it.

What came out of her mouth was, "How do I explain this to my landlord?"

Sam laughed. Really laughed.

Epilogue

Erin hadn't expected to sleep, but she had, since she opened her eyes to sunshine around the edges of the curtains. A new nurse was at her bedside, wanting a temperature and blood pressure, neither of which had anything to do with her injuries. She also heard footsteps in the hall that sounded like a man's.

The nurse was just brushing aside the curtain when Sam walked in.

"Oh, thank goodness!" Darn it, Erin's lips were still swollen on one side, so she didn't sound quite right. "You didn't bring Toby?"

"No, although I'm sure he's gotten the Hillyards up by now," he said drily. "I thought about stopping, but I wanted to talk to you first."

Oh, heavens—what now?

She'd deluded herself yesterday to think she'd remain at home for all the hubbub. The EMT decided she was concussed and should see a doctor and probably have an MRI. In fact, the EMT was right, but the doctor didn't think the concussion was serious and believed Erin could go home this morning.

Toby had been unhappy but okay when he realized he couldn't go with her, but he then threw a rare fit because Sam wouldn't be able to stay with him, either. It was Erin who suggested Andrea Hillyard, the kind next-door neighbor Toby liked well. After all the gunshots fired in Erin's garage, Andrea and Darren wouldn't be surprised.

Now, she said cautiously, "Is this bad?"

"No." Creases deepened on Sam's forehead. "We have a name now. Sawyer Wilkins. And yes, he's the guy who got so pushy at the antique mall that day. His fingerprints matched the ones taken at multiple crime scenes. There are a lot of families who are going to be relieved to know he can't hurt anyone else."

"Because I killed him."

"If you hadn't, I'd have had to take him down. Don't feel any regret for a monster like him."

She bit her lip—*ow!*—and nodded. "Is that it?"

A glint of humor showed in Sam's brown eyes. "I don't know what you're thinking, unless you imagine the landlord has evicted you."

She wrinkled her nose. That was about the only part of her face that didn't hurt. "He might."

"Can I sit down?" Sam had been ignoring the chair, his eye on the bed, and she scooted over to give him room. He engulfed her hand in his much warmer one. The connection felt amazing. "Maybe it's time we told your landlord the truth," Sam suggested, then went entirely still, even his expression shutting down. Was he nervous? "I'm, ah, hoping you might want to shift your operation to my place, anyway. I have some empty outbuildings. Plenty of extra bedrooms. Horses, too."

"That's...kind of jumping ahead of yourself," she managed to say, although her heart had taken a giant leap.

"Yeah." Smiling as if he couldn't help himself, Sam bent down and pressed a warm, soft kiss on her forehead. "But just so you know, I'm ready anytime you are. Everything that has happened stinks, except I met you two."

"And we met you," she had to say.

"So you did."

She searched his face. "Toby won't bring back bad memories?"

He shook his head. "Only good ones, and that's okay. Trying to forget didn't work. Like I told you, I've quit seeing Michael in Toby, anyway. I've…come to love him, too."

"Too?"

He still looked worn today, as if he'd aged yesterday when he must have feared he'd lose her…*and* Toby. Left with a body to explain, Sam wouldn't have gotten much sleep last night, either. He certainly hadn't shaved this morning, which was fine; she liked his stubble.

"I started falling for you from the beginning," he said, some extra grit in his voice. "I worked through my doubts faster than I would have expected to. There's nothing more I want than to marry you. I'd like to adopt Toby, too."

Without warning, tears blurred her vision.

He took her in his arms and murmured, "I'm sorry! I didn't mean to upset you. If you don't feel the same…"

Erin swiped her face against his clean T-shirt and looked up. "Of course I feel the same! I'm happy!"

When he gently kissed her swollen mouth, she felt the vibration of his chuckle.

From that first day when he'd strolled toward her where she sat on the asphalt hugging Toby, a possibility had unfurled in her. She hadn't consciously thought, *I could love this man*, but the fall hadn't been far.

He was right. A lot that happened had been terrifying, but she and Toby had found Sam.

And he'd found them.

* * * * *